D1447568

Heather from Nannie
Christmas _ 1959.

THE BOBBSEY TWINS
AT SCHOOL

*"Bert . . . made the great big teeth . . . there stood the biggest grinning
pumpkin the Bobbseys had ever seen"*

The Bobbsey Twins at School

By

LAURA LEE HOPE

Published by

WORLD DISTRIBUTORS (MANCHESTER) LIMITED

LONDON – MANCHESTER

ENGLAND

THE BOBBSEY TWINS BOOKS

By Laura Lee Hope

First impression 1955
Reprinted   1955
Reprinted   1956
Reprinted   1957
Reprinted   1958

CONTENTS

CHAPTER I

A CIRCUS TRAIN

"WE'RE almost home! Only half an hour to Lakeport!" Nan Bobbsey glanced at her wrist-watch and then looked out of the window of the speeding train.

"We've been away two months," her twin brother Bert remarked. "Things at home will seem strange to us."

Bert and Nan sat opposite each other in facing seats. Beside them were their younger brother and sister, Freddie and Flossie. Freddie pressed his nose against the windowpane. It was starting to get dark, and here and there a light from a house blinked in the distance.

"If we're near home," said Freddie, "I'd better tell Snoop."

The little boy stood on the seat, reached overhead to the luggage-rack and got a basket. He set it down and lifted the lid a little bit.

7

"Snoop, Snoop!" he called softly. "We'll be home in a little while. Then you won't have to be shut up any more. You can chase a mouse in our garden!"

The black kitten inside the basket answered with a purr, as if to say he had had enough of the country and the seaside, and would be glad to get back to the big Bobbsey home in Lakeport. Freddie closed the lid and set the basket back up on the rack.

"When does school open, Nan?" Flossie asked. The little girl had been talking about school for the past few days, because she and Freddie were going into the first grade.

"In two weeks," said Nan, smiling.

"Oh, what fun!" Flossie exclaimed.

"I'll say so," Bert said. "I'll see all my friends again. I wonder what Charley Mason did this summer?"

"Probably sailed his boat on the lake," Nan replied.

She meant Lake Metoka, which was not far from the Bobbsey home. Mr. Bobbsey owned a large boathouse on the lake, and several boats.

"We're going to have fun on the lake with our class," said Bert. "Remember Mr. Tetlow's promise?"

Nan did, and when Freddie asked her what

the promise was, Nan told how their principal had promised to take Nan and Bert's class on a boat picnic across the lake after the winter term opened.

"We're going to the woods to study wild bird life," said Nan enthusiastically.

"And our school's going to beat them this year!" Bert declared.

"The birds?" Nan asked, laughing.

"Oh, no," said Bert. "I'm thinking about our school basketball team. We're going to beat Centre School just like we did last year."

"If Danny Rugg doesn't get too rough and spoil things," Nan said.

"Maybe he turned into a good boy this summer," Flossie remarked.

"If that's possible!" Bert declared rather doubtfully.

"Gee, I hope so," said Freddie, turning his nose from the window. "Then he won't chase me any more."

All the Bobbseys hoped that Danny Rugg, the school bully, had turned over a new leaf and would not try to make trouble for them, as he had done in the past.

Mr. and Mrs. Bobbsey, the twins' parents, who were sitting in the next seat, heard their children's talk, and smiled.

"I'm glad they don't mind the holidays are over," whispered Mr. Bobbsey.

As you may know, there were two pairs of twins. Bert and Nan were twelve years of age and Freddie and Flossie were nearly six.

The two older children were tall and slim, and had brown hair and eyes. The younger twins were sturdy and fair, with dimpled cheeks, light hair and blue eyes. All of them were full of fun.

At this moment, the Bobbseys were on their way home from the seaside, where they had visited the home of their Uncle William and Aunt Emily Minturn at Ocean Cliff.

Mrs. Bobbsey glanced out into the growing darkness and said to her husband, "Hadn't you better get some of the bags together, Richard, and tell Dinah we're nearly there?"

"I think I will," he answered, and went up the aisle a little way to where a stout coloured woman was sitting. She was Dinah, the Bobbseys' good-natured cook, who had gone with them to the seaside. When Mr. Bobbsey spoke to her she arose and began to collect the twins' belongings.

"Mother," said Flossie, "I'm thirsty. May I get a drink?"

"I want one, too," Freddie said. "Come on, Flossie, we'll go together. I can reach the paper cups."

"But I want to drink out of our Ocean Cliff cup," Flossie said. "Mother, may I?"

Flossie was referring to a beautiful silver cup which had been given to the Bobbseys just before they had left the seaside. It was a gift from a family whom they had helped, and the Bobbseys would always treasure it.

"All right," said Mrs. Bobbsey, "but be careful not to drop it." She reached into her bag for the lovely cup.

"I'll carry it," Freddie said. "I'm the biggest."

"You are not," declared his sister. "I'm just as big."

"Well, anyhow, I'm a boy," went on Freddie, and Flossie could not deny this. "And a boy always carries things for a girl."

"Carry it then," Flossie said, and their mother gave Freddie the cup.

When the little twins approached the water-cooler at the end of the car, Freddie stopped. "Look at that lady!" he whispered excitedly.

In the seat just ahead sat a very, very fat woman, who occupied nearly the whole seat. She was so large that even Snoop would have had a hard time squeezing in beside her.

"She *is* fat," Flossie agreed. "Did you ever see a lady so big before?"

"Only in a circus," Freddie whispered.

"She'd make two Dinahs," Flossie went on.

"No, she wouldn't," Freddie contradicted, "'cause Mummy says there'll never be another Dinah."

The sudden sway of the train nearly made Flossie fall, and she grabbed Freddie.

"Look out!" he cried. "You almost made me drop the cup."

When they reached the water-cooler, Freddie half-filled the cup and held it towards his sister. She drank all the water.

"Do you want any more?" Freddie asked before getting a cupful for himself.

"Just a little," Flossie replied. "I'm hot."

Freddie gave his sister some more water and then took some himself. As he drank, his eyes were constantly upon the fat lady. She noticed him and smiled. Freddie was somewhat confused and looked down.

Just as he did so, there was a shrieking, grinding sound and a jar that shook the whole carriage. The train came to such a sudden stop that almost everybody was thrown from his seat.

The little twins sat down hard in the aisle. Surprised as he was by the sudden jolt, Freddie nevertheless noticed that the fat lady had not budged from her seat. She was too heavy.

"It's a wreck!" cried a man suddenly.

"We're off the track!" shouted another.

"It's an accident, anyhow," came still another voice, and everybody seemed to start talking at once.

Mr. Bobbsey hurried down the aisle to where the twins sat, still dazed. When he found that they were not hurt, he led them back to their seat.

The older twins were already looking out of the window. There were many lights up ahead on the track. Suddenly Bert shouted:

"I see an elephant!"

"And a camel!" Nan cried.

"I want to see!" exclaimed the small twins together, and pushed their faces eagerly against the glass.

"There's a lion in a cage," screamed Flossie.

"It's a circus!" Freddie shouted gleefully, clapping his hands. "Now we can go to a circus!"

Just as he got out of his seat, a guard came into the car.

"There's no danger," he said. "Please keep your seats. A circus train that was running ahead of us went off the track and some of the animals are loose.

"Our engine-driver nearly ran into an elephant. That's why we suddenly stopped. We'll go on as soon as possible. Anybody hurt?"

When the guard was told that nobody in the car had suffered more than a shaking-up, he went into the next coach.

"A circus!" said Bert. "This is a real adventure. Let's watch them catch the animals!"

CHAPTER II

WILD ANIMALS

"BERT, do you think a tiger might come in here?" asked Freddie, remembering all the stories of wild animals he had heard in his short life.

"Or a lion?" questioned Flossie.

"Of course not!" exclaimed Nan. "Can't you see that all the wild animals are still in their cages?"

"Maybe some of 'em are loose," suggested Freddie, and he almost hoped so, as long as they did not bother him.

"I guess the circus men can look after them," said Bert. "May I get off, Dad, and look around?"

"I'd rather you wouldn't, son. You can't tell what may happen."

"Oh, look at that man running after the monkey!" cried Nan.

"Yes, and the monkey's gone up on top of the tiger's cage," added Bert. "Say, this is as good as a regular circus!"

15

Some of the big, glaring lights, used in the tents at night, had been turned on so that the circus and railway-men could see to work, and this glare gave the Bobbseys and other passengers a chance to watch what was going on.

"Look, there's a black-and-white candy cane," giggled Flossie, as a zebra passed by their window.

"Oh, you're right, it does look like one," agreed Nan.

"There's a big elephant!" cried Freddie. "See him push the lion's cage around. Elephants are awful strong!"

The little boy began talking about other circus elephants he had seen, and how he had ridden on a baby elephant one time. Like his brother and sisters, he had had many amusing adventures, and some scary ones, too.

Getting locked in a big department store was one, but that was the time Freddie had found Snoop, the lovely black kitten that was travelling with him now. This adventure took place previously.

The children became very fond of Snoop, who now had grown into a sleek, fat cat, and carried him first to a farm when they went to visit Aunt Sarah and Uncle Daniel Bobbsey, and then on a holiday to the seaside. There was fun in the water, and many jokes were played. Once the small twins were stranded on an island. Later on, a great storm came up, and this gave the twins a chance to see the Coastguard at work saving lives.

Finally the time had come for the Bobbseys to go home, so once more Snoop went on the train with them. And now bigger, wild animals were to be seen right from the train windows!

"Look at that horse!" cried Bert. "He's loose!"

The beautiful white horse was running around excitedly. Two men were trying their best to catch him, yelling:

"Whoa! Whoa!"

Through a field he went, out of sight. Then he reappeared, galloping among the circus people and the cages, as if he had no idea of stopping. Suddenly a woman's voice called out clearly:

"In the ring, Prince!"

"What's that for?" asked Freddie.

A moment later he knew. Prince went back into the field and began to trot in a circle. The woman, dressed in a short skirt, ran out beside him in stockinged feet. Suddenly she jumped to his back and stood up.

"She's a bareback rider!" cried Flossie, clapping her hands.

"She certainly is," spoke up Mrs. Bobbsey from the next seat. "And she has caught Prince!" the twins' mother added, as a man came up and swung a halter and rope over the horse's neck.

"Goody! Goody!" screamed Flossie.

As Prince was led away, the twins turned their attention to the capture of a dozen monkeys who were now climbing around the railway-carriages.

"I wish one would come in here," said Bert.

The others wished so, too, but the nearest they came to the children was outside their window. One monkey, who looked like a bald old man wearing spectacles, paused on the sill a couple of minutes and stuck his tongue out at them. The children screamed with laughter.

The work of getting the escaped monkeys and other animals back into the circus train was going on rapidly. Some of the passengers went outside to watch, but the Bobbseys stayed in their seats and saw the show from the windows. Catching several frisky ponies was the hardest work, but soon even this was accomplished.

When there was nothing more to watch, the wait became very tiresome. Mr. Bobbsey looked about for some railway-man to inquire how much more delay there would be. The ticket-collector came through the carriage.

"When will we start?" asked Mr. Bobbsey.

"Not for some time, I'm afraid," the ticket-collector replied. "The wreck is worse than I thought at first, and some of the carriages of the circus train are across the track, so we can't get by. We may be here another two hours."

"That's too bad. Where are we?"

"Just outside of Whitewood."

"Oh, that's very near home!" exclaimed Mrs. Bobbsey. "Why don't we get out, Richard, walk across the field to the bus-stop, and take a bus home? It won't be far, and we'll be there ever so much quicker."

"Well, we could do that, I suppose," said her husband.

"That's what a number of passengers are doing," said the ticket-collector. "There's no danger in going out now—all the animals are back in their cages."

"Then that's what we'll do," said their father. "Gather up your things, children, and we'll take the bus home. The moon is coming up, and it will be light enough for us to cross the field."

"I'll carry Snoop," offered Freddie.

As he lifted down the basket from the luggage-rack, the little boy let out a yell of dismay.

"What's the matter?" asked Nan.

"Snoop! He's gone! The basket's empty!" Freddie wailed.

Sure enough, the lid was no longer fastened, and the cat was gone.

"My sakes alive!" cried Dinah.

"The lid probably was jarred loose when the train stopped," Bert reasoned. "That's how Snoop escaped."

"But where is he?" wailed Freddie.

A hurried search of the carriage by the children did not locate the pet. Mr. and Mrs. Bobbsey and some of the other passengers then joined in the hunt. But Snoop was nowhere in sight.

"Probably Snoop became frightened when the train stopped so suddenly, and broke loose," said Mr. Bobbsey. "We may find him outside."

"I—I hope an elephant didn't step on him," said Flossie with a catch in her breath.

"Oh-o-o-o! Maybe a tiger or a lion has him!" cried Freddie in horror. "Oh, Snoop!"

"We'll find him for you," said Mrs. Bobbsey, as she opened her bag to get out her gloves. Then she remembered something.

"Freddie, where is our silver cup?" she asked. "You took it to get a drink. Did you give it back to me?"

"No, Mummy, I—I—I must have dropped it when the train bumped us on to the floor," he said. "I'll look for it."

Freddie looked high and low, and his brother and sisters helped him search, but the silver cup could not be found.

"Maybe the fat lady picked it up," Flossie said. "She was near us."

Suddenly they realized the fat lady was no longer in the carriage.

"We'll just *have* to ask her," Freddie declared. "I'm going to see if she's in the next carriage!"

"I'll go with you," said Mr. Bobbsey quickly. "That cup is too valuable to lose."

CHAPTER III

THE SEARCH

WHEN Freddie and his father walked into the next coach, they could plainly see that the fat lady was not sitting there, for no passenger took up more than half a seat!

"Daddy," said Freddie with a sudden idea, "maybe the fat lady belonged to the circus!"

"You might be right," Mr. Bobbsey agreed. "We'll get out and take a look."

With all the twins following, Mr. Bobbsey made his way out of the carriage and along the tracks to the circus train.

"Did you see a fat lady?" Freddie asked a man who was leading a camel.

The man said he had been too busy finding the camel to notice anything else, and walked on. The other children and Mr. Bobbsey asked several circus workers the same question, but none of them had seen the fat lady.

Suddenly Flossie cried out, "Look! Over there!"

"Is it the fat lady?" Freddie asked.

"No. A black cat."

"It must be Snoop!" Freddie shouted gleefully.

They all looked where Flossie was pointing, just in time to see a cat disappear into one of the luggage-vans.

"Wasn't it Snoop, Daddy?" Freddie asked excitedly.

"It might have been," Mr. Bobbsey replied. "I only saw his tail."

"I'll take a look," Bert volunteered.

He ran over to the van and looked inside the big open door. Besides being very dark, the inside of the van was filled with crates and ropes and big sheets of canvas. Finding a cat in there would be difficult. So Bert tried calling.

"Snoop! Snoop!"

There was not even a meow to answer him. The other children tried. Suddenly out bounded a big black cat. But it was not Snoop. This one was twice as big, and growled as it went past. Snoop would never do that!

"We'll give up our search," decided the twins' father. "Cats usually find their way home, anyhow."

This satisfied the small twins, to whom the loss

of Snoop seemed more important than the silver cup. The older twins and their father did not feel the same way. Of course, they hoped that nothing had happened to Snoop, but they were sorry to lose the fine silver cup which had been presented to them so recently. After all, it had a special meaning for them.

When the children and their father reached the coach where Mrs. Bobbsey and Dinah were waiting, Mrs. Bobbsey asked anxiously if they had found the fat lady.

"No," the children all replied at once, and then told their mother how they had decided the fat lady belonged to the circus.

The guard who overheard the conversation said yes, she did belong to the circus. She had missed the show train, and had come on this later one.

"When we stopped, the fat lady got out and went up ahead," said the guard. "Part of the circus train, carrying the performers, was not damaged, and that has gone on. The fat lady is with them."

"Oh, dear!" exclaimed Mrs. Bobbsey. "Can you find her later, Richard?"

"I think so. But it will take some time. I understand the circus is going to Danville—that's a day's run from here. I'll write to the manager there, and ask him if the fat lady knows anything about our silver cup."

Dinah was now standing up, ready to leave the train. The poor woman looked like a porter!

In each hand she held a suitcase. Under each arm was a box. An umbrella dangled from one finger, and she was holding her purse under her chin!

"Oh, my goodness!" exclaimed Mrs. Bobbsey, laughing at the amusing scene.

Bert dashed forward to relieve the coloured woman of some of her burden.

"I'll take Snoop's basket," offered Flossie. "Maybe he'll come home to sleep in it."

Each of the children was given small parcels to carry. Fortunately, it had grown cool and everyone could wear his coat and not have to carry it.

Mr. Bobbsey picked up the other two suitcases, and Mrs. Bobbsey gathered all the odds and ends that were left. When they got outside, Mr. Bobbsey realized for the first time what a tremendous amount of luggage they had with them.

"We never can carry all this to the bus," he said. "We'll be sure to drop some of it or lose it, and besides, these suitcases are mighty heavy." He chuckled. "Mother, you must have brought all the shoes we owned."

Mrs. Bobbsey smiled at his teasing, for of course she had not brought that many shoes, but she realized it would be impossible to carry their luggage so far.

"How would it be," she suggested, "if Dinah and I take the children home and you stay on the train with the luggage?"

Mr. Bobbsey groaned. "I never could get all this stuff off the train alone," he said.

"I'll stay with you," offered Bert.

In the end it was Dinah who made the suggestion which they followed. She brought to their attention that it was supper-time and everyone should eat. Bert and his father could not go without food any better than the rest of them.

"Why don't we all carry the little bundles," she said, "an' leave all this here stuff what a pack-mule ought to be carryin' anyway, on the train. That nice guard can put it off at the Lakeport station."

"A very good idea," said Mr. Bobbsey. "I admit I'm starving."

He spoke to the guard, who was willing to do this. The Lakeport station-master knew the Bobbseys well and would surely take care of the suitcases and large packages until they were called for.

With every one in the Bobbsey party carrying

something small, the family set off across the field towards the bus-stop. The moon was well up now, and there was a good light flooding the fields.

Nan and Bert walked together, talking about the wreck and some of the incidents of catching the circus animals, especially Prince.

Flossie and Freddie were with Dinah, asking her if she thought they would ever see their pet cat Snoop again. They had had him so long that he seemed like one of the family.

"Maybe he ran off and joined the circus," said Flossie suddenly.

"Maybe," spoke her brother. "But he can't do any tricks, so they won't want him in a show."

"He can so do tricks! He can chase his tail and almost grab it."

"That isn't a trick."

"It is so—as much as standing on your head, isn't it, Dinah?" asked Flossie.

"I guess you'd have to rightly say it is," agreed Dinah. "I never heard of trick cats, though—just dogs."

"Well, it isn't a circus trick," declared Freddie. "I meant a circus trick."

"Snoop is a good cat, anyhow," went on Flossie, "and I wish we had him back."

"Oh, so do I!" exclaimed Freddie.

They were walking now through a little patch

of woods. Bert, who was the last one in line, suddenly called out:

"Something is coming after us!"

"Coming after us? What do you mean?" asked his father.

"I mean I've been listening for two or three minutes now to some animal following us."

Flossie and Freddie held tightly to Dinah's skirt.

"Don't scare the children, Bert," said Mr. Bobbsey a bit sternly. "Did you really hear something?"

"Yes, Dad. It's some animal walking behind us. Listen! Don't you hear it?"

They all listened. From down the hard dirt path they all heard the *pit-pat, pit-pat* of footsteps. Was it one of the circus animals that had not been captured?

CHAPTER IV

A NEW PET

MR. BOBBSEY peered through the gloom.

"I can see something," he said. "It's coming nearer."

"Oh, dear!" cried Nan fearfully.

Just then a bark sounded—a friendly bark.

"It's a dog!" exclaimed Mrs. Bobbsey. "Oh, I'm so glad it wasn't—an elephant," and she laughed at her own worries.

"Pooh! I wasn't afraid!" bragged Freddie. "If it was an elephant, I—I'd give him some peanuts, and maybe he'd let me ride home on his back."

"And where'd you get the peanuts?" teased Mr. Bobbsey.

The dog barked louder now, and a moment later he came into sight on a moonlit part of the path. The children could see that he was a big, shaggy white dog. He wagged his tail in greeting as he bounded up to them.

"Oh, how lovely he is!" cried Nan. "I wonder where he belongs?"

As the fine-looking animal came on, Bert snapped his fingers. Instantly the dog stood up on his hind legs and began marching about in a circle.

"What a funny dog!" cried Flossie.

Down on to his four legs dropped the big white dog, and with another wag of his fluffy tail he made straight for Flossie.

"Be careful!" warned Dinah.

"He won't hurt her!" declared Bert. "This is a good dog; anyone can tell that. Here, doggie. Come here!"

The dog barked a little and, coming up to Flossie, again stood on his hind legs.

"That's a good trick," said Mr. Bobbsey. "This dog has been well trained."

"I wish he belonged to us," sighed Nan.

"Maybe we can keep him—especially if we don't find Snoop," suggested Freddie.

The dog seemed to have made great friends with Flossie. She was patting him on the head now, for the animal, after marching about on his hind legs a second time, was down on all fours again.

"Oh, Mummy, he's awful nice!" exclaimed Flossie. "He's just as gentle and just as soft as the toy lamb I used to have."

"Indeed he does seem to be a gentle dog," said

Mrs. Bobbsey. "But come along now. Don't pet him any more, or he may follow us, Flossie, and whoever owns him would not like him to do that."

"Forward—march!" called Freddie, strutting along the moonlit path like a soldier.

The Bobbseys and faithful Dinah started off again towards the distant bus-stop. The dog sat down and looked after them.

"I—I wish we could take him home," said Flossie wistfully, waving to the dog.

The Bobbseys had not gone very far before Nan called out, "Oh, Dad, that dog is following us!"

They all glanced back on hearing this. Sure enough, the big white dog was running after them, wagging his tail joyfully and barking.

"This will never do!" exclaimed Mr. Bobbsey. "Whoever owns him may think we are trying to take him away. I'll drive him back. Go home! Go back!" exclaimed Mr. Bobbsey sternly.

The dog stopped wagging his tail. Then he lay down on the path, and calmly waited, his head between his forepaws.

"He—he looks—sad," said Freddie. "Maybe he hasn't any home, Daddy."

"Of course a valuable dog like that has a home," declared Bert.

"But maybe they didn't treat him kindly, and

he's looking for a new one," suggested Nan hope-fully, as the dog came on again.

"He doesn't seem ill-treated," spoke Mrs. Bobbsey. "Oh, I do wish he'd go back, so we could go on."

"Go back! Go back, I say!" cried Mr. Bobbsey in a loud voice. The dog stopped walking. "I guess he won't follow us any more," said the twins' father uncertainly. "Hurry along now, children. We are almost at the bus-stop."

He turned away from the dog, and the family went on. For a minute or two the dog did not fol-low. But just as the Bobbseys were about to make a turn in the path, up jumped the animal and trotted after them. He was wagging his tail so fast that it seemed as if it would come loose.

"Is he following?" asked Flossie.

"He certainly is," answered Bert, who was in the rear. "I guess he wants us to take him home with us."

"Oh, let's do it!" begged Flossie.

"Please, Daddy," pleaded Freddie. "We haven't got Snoop now, so let's have a dog. And I'm sure we could teach him to do more tricks—he's so smart."

"But how can we take him on a bus?" asked Mrs. Bobbsey. "The conductor wouldn't let us."

"Maybe he would—if he was a nice man,"

suggested Freddie. "We could tell him how we got the dog."

"Well, certainly the dog doesn't intend to lose us," said Mr. Bobbsey with a laugh, after he had tried two or three times to drive the animal back.

"We'll go on a little farther," suggested Mrs. Bobbsey. "By the time we get to the road he may get tired and go back."

"Oh, I hope he doesn't go back!" cried Freddie.

"We want to keep him," said Flossie. "He can run along behind the bus. I'll ask the driver to go slow, Daddy."

The dog seemed to think that he was one of the family now. He came up to each one in turn and let them pat him. His tail kept wagging all the while.

"Well, we'll see what happens," decided Mr. Bobbsey.

Freddie and Flossie walked on, the dog trotting along happily between them.

"There's the bus!" exclaimed Bert, as they went around another turn in the path and came to a road.

In the distance could be seen the headlights of an approaching bus, and a little nearer, the lights of an oncoming car.

"Look out for the car, children!" called Mrs. Bobbsey.

They stood at the side of the road, and as the car came alongside, the man in it slowed down. It was a big car and he was alone in it.

"Well, hallo there!" exclaimed the driver, as the car stopped. "If it isn't the Bobbsey family—twins and all! What are you doing here, Mr. Bobbsey?"

"Why, hallo, Mr. Blake!" exclaimed Mr. Bobbsey, seeing that the driver was a neighbour and the father of one of Freddie's playmates. "Our train was held up by a circus wreck, so we walked across the field to take a bus. We're homeward bound from the seaside.

"Well, well! A circus wreck, eh? Where did you get the dog?"

"Oh, he followed us," said Mrs. Bobbsey.

"And we're going to keep him, too!" exclaimed Flossie.

"And take him in the bus with us," added her twin.

"Let me take you home," offered Mr. Blake. "I have this big empty car. Pile in, all of you, and I'll get you home in no time at all. Come, Dinah, I see you, too," he added.

"Yes, sir, Mr. Blake, I'm here. Can't lose old Dinah!"

"But we lost our cat Snoop and our silver cup," said Flossie.

"And we nearly ran over an elephant," added

Freddie, determined that his sister should not tell all the news.

"Can we bring the dog, too?" asked Flossie.

"Yes, there's plenty of room for the dog," laughed Mr. Blake. "Lift him in."

But the strange dog did not need any lifting. He sprang into the back of the car as soon as the door was opened. The others followed, taking seats in back and front.

"This is lovely," said Mrs. Bobbsey with a sigh of relief. "And very kind of you, Mr. Blake."

"I'm only too glad I happened to meet you. Are you children comfortable?"

"Yes!" chorused Freddie and Flossie.

"And the dog?"

"We're holding him so he won't jump out," explained Flossie.

"No fear of that!" said their father dryly.

On went the car. With Nan and Bert telling the adventures of the day, the journey seemed very short. Soon the Bobbsey home was reached.

"The lights in our house are on!" exclaimed Nan, seeing a friendly yellow glow from one of the windows.

"I guess my hubby Sam," said Dinah, "has the house all ready for us."

"It's good to be back again," said Mrs. Bobbsey, getting out of the front seat.

"Here we are!" cried Mr. Bobbsey, as Sam came out on the porch to greet them. "Come, Flossie—Freddie—we're home."

Flossie and Freddie did not answer. They were fast asleep, their heads on the shaggy back of the big white dog.

CHAPTER V

FUNNY TRICKS

WHILE Mrs. Bobbsey put the small twins to bed, Bert and Nan led the dog into the barn behind their house. It was used now as a garage. Nan spread an old quilt in one corner and the beautiful dog lay down on it. He seemed to know that he was to stay there and wagged his tail contentedly.

Then Bert and Nan closed the door and hurried into the house for a very late supper. Directly afterwards they went to bed, planning to get up early the next day to play with their new pet.

But Flossie and Freddie arose first and, after dressing quickly, they asked their mother where the dog was. When she told them, they hurried to the barn.

Freddie opened the door and out bounded the big white dog, barking in delight, and almost knocking the twins down.

"What shall we call him?" asked Freddie.

"Maybe we'd better name him Snoop, like our cat. I guess Snoop is never coming home."

"No, we mustn't call him Snoop," said Flossie. "Some day our cat might come back, and he'd want his own name again. We'll call our dog Snap, 'cause see how his eyes snap. And when Bert snapped his fingers last night, the dog stood up."

"That's a good name," decided Freddie. "Snoop and Snap. I wonder if we can make Snap stand on his hind legs the way he did last night?"

"Ask him to do it," Flossie suggested.

"Stand up!" Freddie shouted.

At once the dog, with a bark, stood up on his hind legs and walked around. The children laughed.

"I wonder if we can make him do any other tricks?" asked Flossie.

"I'm going to try," said her brother. "What trick do you want him to do?"

"Make him lie down and roll over."

"All right," spoke Freddie. "Now, Snap, lie down and roll over!"

At once the big dog did so, and then sprang up with a bark and a wag of his tail, as much as to ask:

"What shall I do next?"

"Oh, isn't he bee-yoo-tiful!" cried Flossie. "I wonder who taught him those tricks?"

"Let's see if he can do any more," said Freddie. "There's a barrel hoop over there. Maybe he'll jump through it if we hold it up."

"Oh, let's do it!" cried Flossie, as she ran to get the hoop.

Snap barked at the sight of it, and capered about as though he knew just what it was for and was pleased at the chance to do more of his tricks. The hoop was so large that Freddie could not hold it steady. So Flossie took hold of one side. When they were in position, Freddie called:

"Come on now, Snap. Jump!"

Snap barked, ran back a little way, turned around and raced forward. He jumped into the air and shot straight through the hoop, landing quite a way off.

"My gracious sakes alive!" called a voice. It was Sam, who had come out to work in the garden. "That's a regular circus trick—that's what it is!"

Sam held a stick in his hand. Before he knew what was happening, Snap raced up and jumped over the stick.

"Oh, look!" cried Flossie.

"Another trick!" exclaimed Freddie.

"My goodness!" cried Sam. "That beats anything I ever saw!"

Snap ran about barking in delight. He seemed happy to be doing tricks.

"Let's go tell Daddy and the others," said Freddie. "They'll want to know about this."

Mr. Bobbsey had not yet gone to his office at the big lumber-yard he owned. He listened to what the little twins had to tell him about Snap, who lay on the lawn. As before, Freddie said he might have come from the circus train.

"But we can keep him, can't we?" begged Flossie.

"Hmm! I'll have to see about that," said Mr. Bobbsey slowly. "I suppose the circus people will want him back, for he must be valuable. Perhaps some clown trained him."

"But if we can't have Snoop, our cat, we ought to have a dog," asserted Freddie.

"I'll try to get Snoop back," said Mr. Bobbsey. "I'll have one of my men go down along the tracks today and inquire of the railway-men. Since Snoop hasn't come back here, maybe he's wandering about down there."

"And don't forget," Mrs. Bobbsey reminded him, "to get in touch with the circus and find out from that fat lady if she knows anything about our silver cup."

Later that morning Bert was out in the front garden, watering the grass with a long hose, when along came Danny Rugg. He stopped. Bert heaved a sigh, wondering what was going to happen.

Danny went to the same school as Bert, but few of the boys and none of the girls liked Danny. He was often rough, and would hit them or want to fight, or would play mean tricks.

"Hallo, Bert!" exclaimed Danny, leaning on the front gate. "I hear you have a trick circus dog here."

"Who told you?" asked Bert.

"Oh, Jack Parker. He says you found him."

"He found us," explained Bert, spraying a bed of geraniums. "He followed us after the circus wreck."

"Well, you took him all the same. I know who owns him, too, and I'm going to tell the man that you took him."

"Oh, is that so?" asked Bert. "Well, we think he belongs to the circus, and my father is trying to find out about it, so you needn't trouble yourself."

"He doesn't belong to any circus," went on Danny. "That dog belongs to Mr. Peterson, who lives over in Millville. He lost a trick dog, and he advertised for it. He's going to give a reward. I'm going to tell him and get the money!"

"You can't take our dog away!" cried Freddie, running up. "Don't you dare, Danny Rugg!"

"Yes, I will!" exclaimed Danny, who often teased the smaller Bobbsey twins. "You won't have that dog after today."

"Don't mind him, Freddie," said Bert in a low voice. "He's trying to scare you."

"Oh, I am, eh?" cried Danny. "I'll show you what I'm trying to do. I'll tell on you for keeping a dog that doesn't belong to you, and you'll be arrested—all of you!"

Freddie looked worried, and tears came into his eyes. Bert saw them and became angrier than ever with Danny.

"Don't cry, Freddie," said Bert. "Look, I'll let you squirt the hose, and you can pretend to be a fireman." Freddie loved to play fireman.

The small boy wiped his eyes as he took the nozzle from his older brother. He carefully aimed the water on the flower beds.

"Well, look at Freddie trying to act real big," snickered Danny. "Thinks he's a real fireman!"

"I am, too!" shouted Freddie, now becoming very angry at Danny. He turned around, ready to argue with the big boy, forgetting about the hose in his hand.

"Ugh!" cried Danny, as the full force of the water hit him in the face.

"Oh!" cried Freddie.

Bert grabbed the hose from his little brother and turned it away from the older boy. "He didn't mean to do that, Danny," Bert said. "He forgot about the hose."

"He did it on purpose!" shouted Danny, soaking wet. "I'll pay you back for this, Freddie Bobbsey!"

With that he pushed open the gate and ran towards Freddie.

CHAPTER VI

GOOD NEWS

FREDDIE saw Danny coming and started running towards the front porch.

"Stop, Danny Rugg!" shouted Bert, dropping the hose. "You leave my brother alone!"

The hose swished around the ground like a snake and the next minute Danny got the full spray on his legs and feet.

"You—you quit that!" he gasped, shaking his fist at Bert. "I'll fix you!"

What a sight Danny was! He was now soaking wet from his head to his feet. Water dripped from his hair and his shirt clung to him. He really looked very funny, but of course he did not think so. His face became beet-red, and he rushed at Bert.

Danny was a bit taller and heavier than Bert, and was always ready to fight someone smaller than himself. But what Bert lacked in size, he made up for in courage. He was not at all afraid of Danny, and stood his ground.

Danny halted and glared at Bert, who looked at him without fear. More than once he and the bully had come to blows, and some of the times Bert had won. Once more Danny turned towards Freddie, who had stopped to see what Bert would do.

"I'll get you yet, Freddie Bobbsey!" cried Danny, shaking his fist at the little fellow and running after him as fast as he could.

"Stop!" cried Bert.

But Danny kept on after Freddie, and the little boy was so frightened that he tripped and fell flat on his face. Bert realized Freddie would be pommelled by the bully in another second.

There was only one thing to do. He picked up the hose and turned it full force on Danny. The water hit the bully in the chest and splattered all over him.

"Ow! Stop! That's cold!" Danny cried out.

He halted a few feet from Freddie, then turned and ran towards Bert. But the closer he came, the stronger the water was, and the wetter he got!

Finally Danny decided he had had enough, and slunk off towards home, muttering threats at the Bobbseys.

At that moment Sam came out of the house. He

saw that something out of the ordinary was going on, and called out:

"Anythin' the matter, Bert? You havin' trouble with somebody?"

"Well, I guess it's all over now," said Bert, as he saw Danny turn the corner.

"If you need any help, just remember that I'm around," said Sam, with a wide grin that showed his fine white teeth. "I'll be right handy, indeed I will!"

"All right. Thanks," said Bert, as he went on watering the flowers.

He let Freddie finish the job. Then the small boy played at being fireman. He pretended this bush and that stone was a house on fire and saved them from burning by means of the hose.

His shouting attracted Flossie, who came running out of the house, followed by Snap. She had just had a shampoo and put on clean clothes, because she was going to a birthday party at Susie Larker's.

"Oh, Freddie," said the little girl, "let's make Snap do some tricks. See if he will jump over the stream of water from the hose."

"All right," agreed her brother. "I'll squirt the water out straight, and you stand on one side of it and call Snap over. Then he'll jump."

Flossie tried this, but at first the dog did not

seem to want to do this particular trick. He walked around on his hind legs and saluted, he "said his prayers", and turned somersaults. But he would not jump over the water.

"Come, Snap, Snap!" called Flossie.

Snap raced about and barked. He seemed to be having the time of his life, but he would not jump.

The twins began to wonder if he were afraid of the water, and Flossie told him he need not get wet if he jumped high enough. Freddie even lowered the hose.

"Jump!" he said.

This time Snap leaped. And he kept on playing the game, no matter how high Freddie held the stream. The dog was dripping wet, though.

"Why, he was only fooling," giggled Flossie.

Just then her mother called to her from the window. "You'd better go now, dear, or you'll be late for the party."

"All right," the little girl replied.

She turned towards the street. Snap, thinking the game was over, ran in front of her and shook himself vigorously. Poor Flossie! Her party dress was spotted with muddy water.

"Oh, you bad dog!" she cried out.

To make matters worse, Freddie in the excitement turned the hose in Flossie's direction. She leaped aside to miss the stream, slipped on the wet grass, and lost her balance. She sprawled full length, with her head in a puddle.

"Flossie child, my poor baby! Come to Dinah!" called the cook, running from the house.

Mrs. Bobbsey came out also. What a sight her little girl was!

"You should have known better than to play with water with a party dress on, Flossie. You will have to change completely and dry your hair before you can go."

"And I'll miss the games," wailed Flossie.

She knew it was no one's fault but her own, yet she felt very sorry for herself. With Dinah's help, however—Mrs. Bobbsey had to leave to meet Mr. Bobbsey downtown—Flossie was ready in short order for the party.

"I guess it was just meant to happen," she said to Dinah. " 'Cause you know what? The first time I started, I forgot to take my present for Susie!"

"So you did," said Dinah, seeing the fancy package with a book in it still lying on Flossie's bureau.

"I'll never squirt the hose again when you're dressed up," said Freddie, as his twin came outside. He felt partly responsible.

"Neither will I," said his sister. "Never, never!"

Snap, who was lying in the sun drying off, blinked and wagged his tail. They wondered how much he understood.

"Dogs are awful smart," Freddie told Dinah. "And so are cats. I wish we had Snoop back."

That evening at supper Freddie asked his father if any of the railway-men had seen the cat, but Mr. Bobbsey said none had, and added:

"I'm afraid you'll have to get along without Snoop. He seems to have disappeared for good. But, anyhow, you have Snap."

"But someone may come along and claim him," said Bert. "Danny Rugg says he belongs to Mr. Peterson in Millville."

"Well, I'll call Mr. Peterson on the telephone this evening and find out," said Mr. Bobbsey.

Fortunately for the twins there was no answer, so the lovely dog would remain with them for one more night at least.

"Does that make you feel better, little Fat Freman?" asked his daddy. This was his pet name for Freddie. "And you, too, my Fat Fairy?" he grinned at Flossie.

They both nodded, and went to bed hoping that neither Mr. Peterson nor anyone else would claim Snap.

Mr. Bobbsey tried telephoning Mr. Peterson

once more that evening. Again there was no answer.

As he hung up, Sam came in to say good night. Mr. Bobbsey asked the coloured man if he knew Mr. Peterson from Millville.

"I don't rightly know Mr. Peterson, sir," explained Sam, "but I've heard a lot about him through a friend of mine. You see, Old Joe's Mr. Peterson's gardener. S'pose I call him and see if his trick dog is big and white and shaggy."

Mr. Bobbsey agreed that this was a good idea. So Sam called Old Joe. He learned that the missing dog for which Mr. Peterson had advertised was a fox-terrier. It could hardly answer the description of Snap.

The Bobbseys thanked Sam and said good night.

It was the middle of the night when the Bobbsey household was awakened by the sound of the fire bell, as the big engine raced through their street. Every one heard it and flew to the windows.

"The fire must be near here," Mr. Bobbsey said to his wife. "Guess I'll go take a look. It's a windy night and a fire in my lumber-yard would be very bad!"

As he spoke, a red glare lit up the sky in the direction of the lake, where the yard was.

"It *is* near there!" he said. "I'd better go and find out about it."

He rushed to the telephone and called the fire-station. By this time all the children were in the hall listening. They heard their father say grimly:

"Our boathouse is on fire!"

CHAPTER VII

THE BIG FIRE

"OUR boathouse is on fire!" cried Bert. "Oh, my canoe will burn up!"

"And our lovely sailboat!" exclaimed Nan. "Oh, Daddy, this is horrible!"

"It *is* horrible," her father agreed grimly. "I'd rather lose both those boats than the motor-boat!"

He was already dashing back into his room to dress.

"Please take me. I'm a fireman," said Freddie, pattering after his father in his bare feet.

"Not this time," Mr. Bobbsey replied. Then, seeing the disappointment in his small son's eyes, he added, "If Mother wants to bring you, all right."

Another engine dashed by the Bobbsey house, and the sound of the bell increased. The voices and footsteps of many persons, as they rushed on to the blaze, could also be heard, and there resounded the cry: -

52

"Fire! Fire! The lake's on fire!"

"What do they mean?" asked Flossie fearfully.

Her mother guessed that more than one boat-house must be on fire. Perhaps dry grass was burning. She hoped that the fire would not spread to the near-by lumber-yard.

Bert was dressing quickly in his room. He hoped his father would let him go to the lake. At any rate, he intended to be ready when he made his request, so as not to cause delay.

By this time Mr. Bobbsey had dressed and had started downstairs. Bert raced after him.

"May I come, Dad?" he asked.

Mr. Bobbsey hesitated a moment, then said with a smile, "Well, I suppose so, since you are dressed."

When they reached the street, they could tell that the fire was mounting higher. The wind was blowing hard, sending sparks in every direction. There were many buildings down by the lake, and if the fire should get out of control, there was no telling what might happen.

The Bobbseys' boathouse was a large one, having recently been made bigger, as Mr. Bobbsey was thinking of buying a new boat to use in his business. As he and his son reached the water-front, both of them gasped. Not only was their boathouse on fire, but also those on either side of it, as well as a dock running out into the lake!

The firemen were working furiously, hacking through windows and spraying chemicals on petrol-tanks to keep them from exploding. Huge streams of water were spurting everywhere, not only to drown the flames, but to keep other buildings from catching on fire.

Every few moments there would be a great hissing sound and more white smoke would billow out. Only one side of the Bobbsey boathouse was ablaze as yet.

"Oh, I hope they'll save it!" cried Bert.

"You wait here!" said his father, rushing forward.

"Where are you going?" Bert wanted to know.

"I'm going to see if I can save any of our boats."

When the firemen recognized him, they let Mr. Bobbsey through the lines. They were a little worried about his trying to move the boats. At this moment two of the men who worked at his lumber-yard stepped up.

"We'll help!" they called out.

"Good!" said Mr. Bobbsey.

They rushed around to the front and climbed into the motor-boat. Mr. Bobbsey had brought the key. He quickly started the engine.

One of his helpers grabbed the gunwale of the

sailboat, and the other man grasped the side of Bert's canoe. Together, the three boats pulled out into the lake, safe from the fire.

"Hurrah! Hurrah!" shouted Bert.

The rescue of the boats was just in time. The blazing wall toppled inside. A few minutes later the roof fell in. There was no chance to save the rowboat or anything else in the building. But this loss was small compared to the other boats.

A third engine was working now, and so much water was pumped that no fire could have withstood it for very long. In fact, the three buildings would suffer as much water damage as burned wood.

Mr. Bobbsey moored the boats at the lumberyard and then returned to the fire. By this time the blaze was practically out. One engine continued to throw water on the smouldering sparks. The crowd began to leave now, for there was nothing more to see, and it was chilly.

"My!" exclaimed Bert as his father came to where he had left his son, "it didn't take you long to rescue the boats. That was swell!"

His father smiled. "I couldn't have done it if the firemen hadn't assured me the place would be safe a few more minutes. We have a good fire department. This whole lakeside might have burned."

"Flossie and Freddie and Nan are over there with Mother," said Bert.

They walked to where the four were standing. Freddie was telling a fireman who he was and that he wanted to be a fireman when he grew up.

"I wish I could squirt some water right now," begged Freddie.

"What's that? You want to be a fireman?" asked the man in the rubber coat and big helmet.

"Yes, I do," said Freddie.

"Then come with me, and I'll let you help hold the hose," said the fireman. "I'll look after him," he went on to Mrs. Bobbsey, and she nodded to show that Freddie could go.

What a good time the little fellow had, standing beside a real fireman, and helping throw real water on a real fire! Freddie never forgot that. Of course, it was only one of the small hose lines that he held, but Freddie was very happy just the same.

The fire chief came up to Mr. Bobbsey, who expressed his thanks for the quick work of the firemen in helping him to save his boats.

"Have you any idea what started the fire, Mr. Bobbsey?" asked the chief. "Was the boathouse in use?"

"Not tonight," the twins' father replied. "Did the fire start here?"

"We suspect it did." He held out a partly filled

packet of cigarettes. "These were lying along-side your boathouse," he said. "And near the wall inside were two half-smoked cigarettes of the same brand."

"You found some of these cigarettes in the boat-house?" asked Mr. Bobbsey, astounded. "No one I know smokes this kind. They're Mosswoods."

"The question is, who was smoking?" went on the chief. "In my opinion, a cigarette thrown aside, or perhaps a lighted match dropped in some corner, started this fire."

The Bobbseys looked at one another in bewilder-ment. Who had broken into their boathouse?

CHAPTER VIII

THE BOAT PICNIC

AFTER everybody else had gone home from the fire, the police looked for clues to who had started it, but they could find none. It was still a mystery when school opened a few days later. The twins were eager to go, but were sorry to have the carefree holidays come to an end.

"I think you have had a wonderful holiday," remarked Mrs. Bobbsey at breakfast, "and if Freddie and Flossie are going to do such tricks as they did with the hose the other day, I, for one, shall be glad that you are in school and out of mischief." She added, smiling, "You can't play in first grade like you did in kindergarten. You must study hard now."

"We will," they promised.

The four Bobbseys went off together to school, which was only a few blocks from their home. Mr. Tetlow was the principal.

"Hallo, Nan," greeted Grace Lavine. "I hope I can sit near you this term."

"I do, too," said Nellie Parks. "But maybe we'll have to sit alphabetical."

"Maybe we can be together," said Nan with a smile. "Let's ask the teacher!"

"I'm going to sit with Freddie," declared Flossie. "We have to be together 'cause we're twins."

"Of course," agreed Nan. "Speak to your teacher about it."

Bert was walking in the rear with Charley Mason, when Danny Rugg came around a corner.

"I know what I'm going to do to you after school, Bert Bobbsey!" he called. "You just wait and see!"

"All right—I'll wait," Bert said coolly.

By this time they were at the school, and it was nearly time for the last bell to ring. Danny went off to join some of his particular friends, glaring at Bert as he went.

"What's the matter, Bert?" asked Nan, seeing him in the hall.

"There's nothing the matter."

"Yes, there is," insisted Nan. "I can tell by your face. It's Danny Rugg, isn't it? Bert, is he trying to pick a fight with you again?"

"Well, he said he was going to."

"Oh, Bert, I hope you don't get into a fight."

"I won't, Nan—if I can help it. At least I won't hit first, but if he hits me——"

Bert looked as though he knew what he would do in that case.

"Oh, dear!" cried Nan. "Please be careful."

She had no trouble in getting permission from her teacher for Grace, Nellie, and herself to sit near each other. In a review of the previous year's work, they answered questions promptly and correctly.

Poor Bert did not fare so well. He kept thinking of what might happen between himself and Danny Rugg when school was over, and when his teacher asked him what the Pilgrim Fathers did when they first came to settle in New England, Bert looked up in surprise and said:

"They fought."

"Fought!" exclaimed the teacher. "Why, Bert, they gave thanks for a safe journey."

"Well, I meant they fought the—er—the Indians," stammered Bert.

"Yes, they did fight the Indians later on," admitted the teacher, "but that wasn't what I meant."

She called on another pupil and Bert was relieved. He did not see Danny Rugg at the midday break when the Bobbsey twins and the other children went home to lunch.

But when school was over in the afternoon, and Bert was outside talking to Charley Mason about a new way of making a kite, Danny Rugg came up. He was accompanied by several of his friends.

"Now I'll fix you, Bert Bobbsey!" snarled Danny, as he advanced with doubled-up fists. "You're going to wish you hadn't squirted that hose on me! I said I'd get even with you, and now I'm going to do it!"

"I didn't start this, Danny," said Bert quietly, "but if you want to make something of it, I will, too."

"Huh! He's afraid!" sneered Jack Westly, one of Danny's friends.

"Yes, he's a coward!" taunted Danny.

"I'm not!" cried Bert stoutly.

"Then see how you like that!" exclaimed Danny, and he gave Bert a push that nearly knocked him down. But Bert regained his balance and struck Danny on the shoulder.

"There! He hit you back!" cried one boy.

"Yes, go in there, Danny, and beat him!" said another.

"Oh, I'll fix him now," boasted Danny, circling around Bert.

Bert was carefully watching. He did not want to let Danny get the better of him if he could help it.

Danny struck Bert on the chest, and Bert hit the bully on the cheek. Then Danny jumped forward swiftly and tried to give Bert a blow on the head. But Bert stepped to one side, and Danny slipped to the ground. Bert waited warily while Danny picked himself up.

"Look out! Here comes Mr. Tetlow!" cried Jack.

This was a signal for all the boys, even Danny and Bert, to run, for, though school was over, it was against the rules to fight on the school grounds.

"Anyhow, you knocked him down, Bert," said Charley Mason, as he ran off with Bert. "You won!"

About a week later Mr. Tetlow announced to the upper classes in assembly that on the following day they would have the promised boat picnic.

"That's great," said Bert to Nan, as they walked back to their classroom. "I hope Dinah fixes us a good lunch."

"She will," smiled Nan.

The pupils had been looking forward to the trip since the spring before, and all were in high spirits as they assembled on the public dock on Lake Metoka, carrying their lunches.

"Here's the boat, all ready to go," Bert said to Nan, looking at the *White Star*.

"And it has a fresh coat of paint," Nan pointed out.

Indeed, the excursion boat was decked out as if for a festive occasion. It was painted white, with red trim, and glistened in the sunlight.

The boat could carry a hundred passengers, but the school class, along with teachers and a few parents, numbered not more than fifty, so there was plenty of room for play.

"All aboard!" suddenly came a shout from Mr. Tetlow.

The gangplank had been lowered and the children filed on board. In a few minutes the *White Star* gave two long whistles, sending a cloud of steam into the air, as it moved slowly away from the dock.

"Oh, look! There's your burned boathouse!" shouted Charley Mason to Bert.

"Yes," Bert replied sadly, "it sure is a sorry sight! But Dad saved our boats."

"The police are still looking for the one who set it afire," Nan spoke up.

"I'll bet when they find him, they'll put him in jail," Charley said.

"They sure will," Bert agreed.

"What'd you say?" suddenly asked a voice behind Charley. It was Danny Rugg.

"We were talking about the fire in the Bobbsey boathouse."

"Oh, that!" said Danny. "It should have been burned down long ago. Ugliest boathouse on the lake!"

Bert's face grew red when he heard this. He knew an architect had planned his father's boathouse and it was a good-looking one. Danny was only trying to start another fight.

"Don't mind him, Bert," Nan said.

"Yes," agreed Charley. "Let's not start an argument on the class picnic."

"I'll start an argument whenever I please," Danny said hotly.

"Still sore about your soaking with the hose?" Bert needled him.

"Wait until I get my hands on that stupid little brother of yours," said Danny.

"Freddie's not stupid, and you'd better not touch him!" Bert warned him.

"Then maybe you'd like to take a punch instead," snapped Danny.

He cocked his fist and swung at Bert, but fanned the air. He had swung so hard that he lost his balance and sprawled on to the deck. As he did so, a packet of Mosswood cigarettes fell from his pocket.

"Oh!" exclaimed several pupils who were looking on.

Danny quickly snatched up the packet and thrust

it into his pocket. Then he hurried along the deck until he came to a door and disappeared inside the cabin.

"Mr. Tetlow ought to know about this," a girl suggested, but Bert declared he would not tell on Danny.

"Say, maybe some kids were smoking and set your boathouse on fire," Charley suggested.

Bert was thinking the same thing. Mosswood cigarettes! Maybe *Danny* was responsible.

"Do you think it could have been Danny?" Nan asked excitedly.

"We shouldn't accuse anybody until we really know," Bert said. "But I'm going to keep an eye on Danny Rugg!"

By this time the *White Star* was well out on the lake, and there were more interesting things to talk about than Danny, who was still keeping out of sight. The children played games and admired the beautiful scenery of the hills that surrounded the lake. Soon it was time for lunch, and what fun everybody had! Lunch kits popped into view all over the deck, and Mr. Tetlow stood behind a table, handing out bottles of lemonade.

It was late in the day when the boat returned to its dock with the tired but happy children. When Bert arrived home with Nan, he told his father about Danny and the cigarettes.

"Hmm," said Mr. Bobbsey. "I wonder——"
But he said no more, because at that moment
Freddie and Flossie bounced into the house full of
stories about their adventures in school that day.

When they had finished talking, Mr. Bobbsey
said he had two important announcements to
make, one about Snap, the other about the circus.

CHAPTER IX

IN THE WOODS

"I FINALLY found out that Snap doesn't belong to anybody around Lakeport," Mr. Bobbsey said.

"Hurrah! Hurrah!" shouted Freddie, dancing around. "Snap is ours!"

"I wouldn't say that exactly," Mr. Bobbsey replied. "I'm still trying to get in touch with the circus about Snap, and about the fat lady and the silver cup, too. But we won't be able to find out anything for some time."

"Why not?" asked Bert.

"Because the circus has sailed for Puerto Rico and Cuba!" his father replied.

Freddie hugged Snap, sure that the trick dog was to be theirs for a long while. Then Flossie had a turn. The older twins were also glad to hear that Snap would remain with them.

"Did you hear that, old fellow?" said Bert, patting him.

The next few days were quiet ones for the twins. Danny Rugg did not even speak to Bert, either because he was afraid the principal had seen him trying to fight Bert, or because of what the children had seen fall from his pocket. At any rate he caused no trouble.

School days went on, and the pupils settled down to their work for the long winter term. The thought of the snow and ice that would come a little later gave Bert an idea. One day he said on the way home from school:

"Charley Mason and I are going to make a big bob-sled this year. It's going to carry ten fellows."

"And no girls?" asked Nan with a smile. She was walking along with her brother, Grace Lavine, and Nellie Parks.

"Sure, we'll let you girls ride once in a while," said Charley, as he caught up to his friend. "But you can't steer."

"I steered a bob once," said Grace. "It was Danny Rugg's."

"Pooh! His is a little one alongside the kind Charley and I are going to make!" exclaimed Bert. "Ours will be hard to steer, and it's going to have a siren on it to warn folks to get out of the way."

"That's right," agreed Charley. "And we'd better start building it right away, Bert. It may snow before we finish!"

"It doesn't feel like snow now," Nan laughed. "It's very warm. It feels more like ice-cream-cone weather."

"If you'll come with me, I'll treat you all to some," offered Nellie. "I have part of my birthday money left."

"Oh, but there are five of us!" cried Nan, counting. "That's too many for you to treat, Nellie."

"I have a dollar, and really it's hot today."

It was warm, being the end of September, with Indian summer near at hand.

"Well, let's go to Johnson's," suggested Nellie. "They have the best ice-cream."

"Here come Flossie and Freddie!" exclaimed Nan. "We can't take them, Nellie. That would mean——"

"Of course I'll take them!" exclaimed Nellie generously. "Come on!" she called to the small twins. "We're going to buy ice-cream cones."

"Oh, goody!" cried Flossie. "I was just wishing for one."

"So was I," added her brother. "I'm awful hot."

"We'll ask you to our Hallow-e'en party," Flossie went on. "We're going to have one, you know!"

"Oh, are we really, Flossie?" asked Nan. "I hadn't heard about it."

"Mummy just told us we could, but she told me not to tell. I don't care; I wanted Nellie to know, 'cause she's going to treat us to cones."

"I'd love to come," Nellie replied. "Now let's hurry. It's getting hotter and hotter."

They all trooped into the shop while she purchased the cones. The older children chose chocolate, but Flossie and Freddie liked vanilla best.

As the children walked up the street eating them, Bert and Charley began talking about the bob-sled they were going to make. When they reached the Bobbsey house, the two boys went to the loft of the garage, where they were going to build it.

The girls, with Flossie and Freddie, stopped on the Bobbsey lawn, where there were several comfortable chairs. They sat in the shade of the trees, and Freddie had Snap do some of his tricks. The visitors laughed and said he was wonderful.

"Can he jump through a hoop covered with paper, like dogs in the circus?" asked Nellie.

"Oh, we never thought to try that," said Freddie. "I'm going to make one." He hurried into the house. "Dinah," he called, "I want some paper and paste to make Snap do a trick."

"Land sakes, child! I hope you're not goin' to make a kite and give Snap a ride like you did poor little Snoop!"

"No, we're not going to do that," laughed the little boy. "We're going to cover a paper hoop and have Snap jump through it."

"My goodness!" cried Dinah. "What will you be up to next?"

Nevertheless, she thought the trick would be a good one if it would work. She hunted for a tube of paste, but there did not seem to be any in the house.

"I'll fix you some flour-and-water paste," offered the kindly cook. "It'll hold just as good."

She mixed a cupful and found a hoop from a barrel, while Freddie located a large sheet of red tissue paper left from Christmas. He took them all to the back porch, hoping to surprise the other children with a really fine paper hoop. Ten minutes later Dinah came out to see how the little boy was getting along.

"My goodness!" she cried. "All the paste's on your clothes, 'stead of on the paper!"

This was indeed the sad truth. Besides, the tissue paper was torn in several places.

"I—I guess I'm not a very good paster," said Freddie. "Maybe I just ought to be a fireman. I'll ask Nan to make the hoop for Snap."

He went for another piece of the red tissue and Dinah made more paste. Then he carried them and the barrel stave to the front lawn.

"Please paste these together, Nan," begged Freddie. "I can't."

"All right," said his sister.

Even for Nan, covering a hoop with paper was not so easy as she thought it would be. Grace and Nellie helped her, but sometimes the wind would blow the paper away just as they were ready to fold it around the rim of the hoop.

"What are you doing?" asked Bert, as he and Charley came from the garage. They had had to stop work on their bob-sled, as they could not find a long enough plank for the seat. They would get one from Mr. Bobbsey's lumber-yard.

"We're going to have Snap do a circus trick," explained Freddie. "Only we can't seem to get the hoop made."

"I'll do it," offered Bert.

As he and Charley had often pasted paper on their kite frames, they had better luck, and soon the hoop was ready.

"Come, Snap!" called Freddie.

It had been decided that he and Flossie would be the ones to hold the hoop for the dog to leap through. Snap, always ready for fun, jumped up from the grass and frisked about, barking loudly.

"You hold him, Nan," directed Bert. "I'll go

over on the other side of the hoop and call him.
Then you let him go. He ought to jump right
through the paper."

Flossie and Freddie were so excited they could
hardly hold the hoop steady. When Bert gave the
signal, Nan let the dog go. He raced for the hoop
and leaped up.

Rip! Tear! The paper burst and Snap sailed
through the hoop just as a trained dog often does
in the circus, sometimes while on the back of a
galloping horse.

"Oh, that was wonderful!" cried Grace.

"Let's make another hoop!" said Flossie.

"Let's make a lot of 'em, and have a circus with
Snap, and charge money to see him, and have lots
of money to buy ice-cream!" suggested Freddie
wildly.

The others laughed, but they did make more
hoops, and Snap seemed to enjoy jumping through
them.

Bert and Charley left for the lumber-yard and
consulted Mr. Bobbsey on the best kind of wood to
use for the seat of their bob-sled.

"I'd use something that's sturdy but not top-
heavy," said Mr. Bobbsey. "A twelve-foot ash
board, an inch and a quarter thick. I'll have Sam
bring it up when he comes home."

Bert's father also told them where to obtain thin

strips of sheet-iron for runners, and the boys went off to get them. They worked on the bob-sled every afternoon after school, sawing, whittling, and fitting the sections together.

"Whew!" said Bert one day. "I guess it will snow before we get this thing built!"

The weather remained mild, however, and at times it was hard for the schoolchildren of Lakeport to keep from looking out of the windows and wishing they might be on the lake or in the woods instead of in class.

One day word was sent to Flossie and Freddie's room, and to all the other of the lower grades, that if the weather was clear the following morning, the children would go on a Nature walk and picnic in Ward's Woods.

"Goody!" cried Flossie and several others, though they were not supposed to burst out in the classroom.

The teacher merely smiled. Secretly she was glad to have such a pleasant outing herself!

Next morning every one of the smaller boys and girls came to school with a lunch. Dinah had packed Freddie's and Flossie's together.

"Oh, we'll have a fine time!" cried Freddie, dancing about the school-yard.

Eleven o'clock came, and with the teachers at the head of their classes, the pupils started off for the woods. The Bobbsey twins were near the end of the line as the hikers reached the trail among the trees.

Suddenly Freddie was nearly knocked over by something jumping on him.

"Snap!" he cried. "How'd you get here?"

"Oooh!" said Flossie. "What will our teacher say?"

CHAPTER X

TWO SNAKES

"SNAP, SNAP!" whispered Freddie and Flossie frantically. "Go home before Miss Burns sees you!"

But the excited dog leaped about, panting, and did not go home.

"Oh, why did you come here, Snap?" Flossie asked.

Snap lifted his head and barked three times, as if to say he had seen the children going for a walk and wanted to come, too. Miss Burns heard him and came back. To the twins' relief, she smiled and patted Snap.

"Whose dog is this?" she asked.

"Ours," spoke up Freddie, over his fright now. "His name's Snap and he does tricks."

"That's very nice," said Miss Burns, "but I don't think he should come along. Will Snap go home if you tell him to?"

The twins said they would try to make him go back, but every time they said, "Go home, Snap," the dog would bark and lick their hands. He even sat up in front of Miss Burns as if to say, "Please take me."

"Well, he won't go home," sighed Flossie.

The teacher said she thought it would be all right for him to stay if the children kept Snap near them. So everybody skipped happily along the woodland path, singing little songs they had learned in school and watching for strange birds.

Snap was having a wonderful time, sniffing at rabbit scents and dashing in and out of the bushes. It was not long before Freddie and Flossie found themselves lagging behind, trying to keep track of Snap.

Suddenly they saw a big boy step from behind a tree. He was Danny Rugg.

"Hey, what are you doing here?" he asked gruffly.

"We're on a picnic," Flossie replied. "And why aren't you in school?"

"I'm ah—sick today," Danny answered. "My mother sent me off to walk in the woods for some fresh air. You say you're on a picnic?"

"Yes," Freddie replied. "The children who didn't go on the boat ride came today."

"Who said you could bring your dog?" Danny asked. "Dogs aren't allowed on school picnics. I'll take him with me. And I'll train him so he'll mind."

Danny picked up a stick. Snap growled and showed his teeth.

"See!" cried Danny. "He's vicious!"

"He is not, Danny Rugg," Flossie said. "He only growled because you acted mean to him. Now you leave us alone, or I'll tell our teacher."

"Pooh! Think I care?"

With that Danny raised the stick and approached Snap. Again the dog growled angrily. He was not used to being treated this way.

"Look out, Danny," Freddie warned, "or he may jump on you and knock you down and bite you—unless I tell him not to."

"I'm not afraid of him," cried Danny, more arrogant than before. "I'll get a bigger stick, and then we'll see what happens."

While he looked about for one, Flossie grasped Freddie's hand.

"Oh, don't let him beat Snap!" she pleaded.

"I won't," Freddie said bravely, standing alongside the shaggy white dog.

By this time Danny had found a big branch. He approached the twins and their dog menacingly.

"*Now* I'll take him with me," he said.

As he held the stick over his head, a voice suddenly came from the woods.

"What's going on here?" It was Miss Burns, coming back along the path. "We've looked all over for you," she said. Then, noticing Danny, who had tried to hide behind a tree but had not succeeded, she added, "What are you doing here? This picnic is not for big boys. You should be at school."

"My mother said I could stay away from school today," Danny said, "and besides, I've got to see that this dog goes home."

"I've already said Snap could come on the picnic," the teacher said. "Now you run along and don't bother these children."

Danny did not say any more. He just scowled at the twins and hurried back down the path. He knew Miss Burns would **report** him to Mr. Tetlow for playing truant.

After Danny had gone, the Bobbseys rejoined their friends and all went on towards the grove in the woods, where the picnic was to be held. There was laughing and shouting and much fun on the way, in which Snap shared.

Each teacher pointed out trees and bushes as they went along. The boys and girls told what they were, if they recognized them. Miss Burns was very proud of her class, who knew oak and pine trees, and barberry and huckleberry bushes, even though there were no berries on them.

The children also gathered pretty leaves. Once Freddie saw a lovely red oak leaf on the far side of a shallow brook. He tried to cross the brook by stepping on some stones. They were covered with moss, and suddenly Freddie slipped.

Splash!

The poor little twin sat down in the water. He got up quickly and waded to the shore.

"Oh, dear," said Miss Burns.

Fortunately Freddie had on heavy trousers and by wiping them off quickly, the water did not soak through. Miss Burns told him to take off his sandals and socks and go barefoot for a while until they dried.

Finally the children reached the grove. It was in a wooded valley, with hills on either side, and a spring of clear, cold water in the middle, where everybody could get a drink. And that always seems to be what is most wanted at a picnic—a drink of water.

Before giving the children free time in which to play, Mr. Tetlow called them all together for instructions. He warned them that they should not go out of the little valley, and that when he blew a whistle they were to come back to that spot.

"And now," he said with a smile, "have fun. Play any games you wish, and eat your lunches any time you like."

When he finished talking, all the children shouted in glee and scampered in every direction.

Freddie took hold of Flossie's hand, leaned close to her, and whispered in her ear, "Mr. Tetlow said we could eat any time. I'm awful hungry, so let's eat our lunch now."

"I'm hungry, too," Flossie replied, agreeable to Freddie's idea.

The children found a nice grassy spot under an oak tree, and opened the wonderful lunch Dinah had prepared for them—surprise sandwiches neatly wrapped in wax paper.

"What's in 'em, do you s'pose?" asked Freddie.

"Oh, look," Flossie giggled. "Lots of other children are eating their lunches, too."

She and Freddie were not the only ones who were hungry after their hike into the woods!

Snap lay down on the ground beside the twins and watched them eat. Once he came and sniffed hopefully at the lunch.

"Snap must be hungry, too," Flossie said. "Here, Snap!"

She took some roast beef from one of her sandwiches and fed it to the dog. Then Freddie gave him a piece of orange layer cake. Snap seemed to enjoy the food as much as the children, and soon there was not a crumb left.

Then the twins went to the spring for a drink. A whole stack of paper cups had been provided by the school. Flossie tried to make Snap drink out of a cup, but this he would not do. Instead, he stood at the edge of the spring and lapped up the water.

"I don't blame him for not using a cup," said Freddie, defending his pet. "He's not a sissy dog!"

"Let's play now," called Teddy Blake, one of the first-graders.

All sorts of games followed, from tag and jumping rope, to blind-man's-buff and hide-and-seek. Snap was constantly at the heels of the twins, so they had to give up trying to hide. He always gave away their hiding-places!

Finally Freddie and Flossie wandered off towards the hill-side, where Flossie had spied some wild asters, one of the last of the late flowers. They picked a number of them, and while Flossie was arranging them in two bouquets, one for Miss Burns, Freddie walked farther up the hill.

The small twin had gone only a short distance when he let out a cry and came running back as fast as his legs would carry him. He looked very much frightened.

"What's the matter?" asked Flossie, looking up. "Did a bee sting you?"

Freddie was so out of breath he could hardly speak. "Up—up there," he gasped. "Up there—a big black one!"

"A black bee?" Flossie asked in surprise.

"No, a snake," Freddie puffed. "I nearly stepped on him!"

At that moment Snap came running up the hill, barking and wagging his tail. He seemed to think he had lost the children, and was telling them how glad he was to find them again.

But Snap did not stop. He continued on up the hill towards the spot where Freddie had been frightened.

"Snap! Don't go up there!" cried Freddie frantically.

"No, don't let him!" pleaded Flossie. "Come back, Snap!"

But Snap had other ideas. He bounded up the hill-side, pausing now and then to dig in the earth. Nearer and nearer he came to the place where Freddie said he had seen the snake.

"Oh, Snap, Snap, don't go there!" cried Freddie, but the dog kept on.

Then suddenly he stopped short, grabbed at something in the grass, and bounded backwards.

"Oh, he's been bitten!" Flossie wailed.

"He's got it!" shouted Freddie.

Snap had something long and black in his mouth. He raced down the hill with it. The twins were so frightened that they could not move.

"Drop it, Snap!" Freddie managed to cry out when the dog had nearly reached them.

Snap obeyed, and stood over the black thing as it lay on the ground. Freddie and Flossie looked down, their eyes growing wide.

"Why—why, it's not a snake at all!" the little boy gasped.

"No, it's an old tree root," laughed his sister. "Oh, Freddie, a tree root scared you!"

"But it's all twisted up like a snake," he replied sheepishly. "I guess you'd have thought it was a snake, too."

"I'm awful glad it wasn't," Flossie said with a sigh of relief.

"So am I," Freddie admitted.

Snap could not understand why the twins had not picked the root up. He had brought it for them to throw, so he could bring it back.

After he had barked a few times, Freddie knew what he meant. He picked up the "snake", and threw it far down the hill. Snap raced after it, brought it back, and dropped it at Freddie's feet.

"You're a good dog," Freddie said as he patted Snap's head. "If this had been a real snake, you would have chased it away and not let it hurt us, wouldn't you?"

If his bark meant anything, Snap was certainly saying, "Yes, sir, you can count on me!"

At that moment Mr. Tetlow's whistle blew. With Flossie carrying her flowers, the twins started back towards the grove. On the way they met Susie Larker, and Flossie started telling her about the funny tree root.

Suddenly Susie said, "Oh, there's a root just like it."

She reached her hand down, but just as she did, the "root" coiled up.

It was a real snake, ready to strike!

CHAPTER XI

HOLDING UP A GAME

"LOOK out, Susie!" Flossie shouted.

The little girl was so frightened she could not move. The snake drew itself up higher and was just about to strike when Freddie shoved her aside. Both of them tumbled on to the grass.

At the same instant Snap jumped for the snake. His powerful jaws grabbed it behind the head, and he shook it with all his might. Then he dropped the snake on to the ground and it did not move.

"Snap killed it!" Freddie cried out.

Mr. Tetlow and several pupils who had heard the shouts came running to see what the excitement was about. As Snap picked up the snake and took it off into the woods, the principal said:

"I saw everything that happened. Freddie, you and Flossie saved Susie from being bitten. You are real heroes, and your dog is, too."

The other children crowded around and started

to cheer. Snap came back from the woods, where he had left the snake. He stood on his hind legs and put his forepaws together, as if clapping too. Everybody laughed.

Mr. Tetlow led the way back to the grove, and blew his whistle again. When all the children had gathered, they started for home. Snap helped keep them in line. He scampered along, first on one side of the path and then on the other, like a wise old sheep-dog guiding a herd of sheep.

When they reached the edge of town, the party broke up, the boys and girls hurrying to their homes. As the twins raced into their driveway with Snap, Freddie and Flossie met Sam. The handyman took off his hat and scratched his head.

"So *you* had Snap. I've been looking for that dog all afternoon!"

Mrs. Bobbsey heard the children and stepped to the front porch. Hearing that Snap had followed Flossie and Freddie, she sighed in relief.

"I'm glad Snap didn't get lost like Snoop," she said. "I was afraid he might even have been stolen."

The twins were sorry every one had been so worried. They told about Snap killing the snake and their mother patted the dog gratefully.

Bert and Nan arrived home from school late that afternoon. Bert had been playing football with the boys, and had had a good time because Danny Rugg was absent from school that day. Nan had been practising with the girls' volleyball team.

"We're going to play a game against Centre School tomorrow," Nan announced that evening. "Our coach hopes all the boys and girls will come and cheer for us."

Nan explained that the game was to be played in the Centre School playground, situated on the opposite side of town from Lakeport School, which they attended.

"I'll cheer for your team!" Freddie exclaimed. "I'll make so much noise that the girls of the other team will drop the ball!"

Nan laughed at her little brother's enthusiasm. Freddie thought Nan was just about the most wonderful big sister in the world and that everything she did was just right.

"I'd like to see you play myself," Mrs. Bobbsey said. "Do you suppose I might come, Nan?"

"Of course," her daughter replied. "Some of the other girls' mothers will be there."

So it was decided that Mrs. Bobbsey would come to school the next afternoon and go with her other children to see Nan play.

The following day was a real Indian summer day, starting out rather cool in the morning, but becoming warm in the afternoon. It was perfect

for the game. Mrs. Bobbsey drove up just as classes were over.

"Look, Mother," Flossie said as she got into the Bobbsey car, "I have a s'prise for you." She made her mother shut her eyes, and then laid several bright-coloured leaves on her lap.

"Oh," said Mrs. Bobbsey, "they are the most beautiful leaves I have ever seen."

Some were as red as the sunset. Others were as gold as pumpkins, and others were just plain green.

"I'll decorate the mantel with these when I get home," her mother said. "Thank you, dear."

By this time all four Bobbsey children were in the car, and their mother set off for the other side of town. Nan was so excited that she could hardly wait to get there and start playing in the contest.

It was not long before they arrived at the Centre School playground. Nan hurried off to meet the volleyball coach and the other girls from the team. Mrs. Bobbsey, Flossie, and the boys found seats on wooden benches to await the start of the game.

In an open grassy spot stood the two volleyball standards, with a big net stretched between them.

"That's just like the net you found at the seaside," Freddie said to Bert.

Indeed, it did look something like the seine Bert had discovered on the sand near Ocean Cliff, only much newer, of course.

"Do they use that for fishing when they're not playing volleyball?" Freddie wanted to know.

Just as Bert was telling Freddie that there weren't enough fish in Lake Metoka to use a net, the girls came running to their places. The game was about to begin.

Then a Miss Perkins, who, Bert said, was the girls' gymnasium teacher at Centre School, came on the field and looked around the grounds. She glanced to where the spectators were sitting on the benches. She seemed more perplexed than ever.

"Has anyone seen the volleyball?" she asked, puzzled.

The people on the benches shook their heads, and the players said they had not seen it.

"It was here just fifteen minutes ago," the gym teacher said. "Where could it have gone?"

Soon everybody was looking under the benches and around the playground. The game could not go on without the ball.

"If we don't find it, we may have to call the game off," said Miss Perkins.

Growing impatient with the delay, Freddie asked his mother if he could play with Flossie while the people were looking for the ball. She said they might, if they did not go out of the playground.

The small twins skipped off to play tag under some big trees at the edge of the field. After they had raced about for a while, Flossie said:

"Let's play in this big pile of leaves, Freddie. Make believe I'm a bear, and you cover me up with leaves for the winter."

Freddie thought this was a wonderful idea. Flossie jumped into the leaves, which had been raked off the field, and Freddie threw handfuls of them on top of her. Soon nothing could be seen of Flossie.

"Don't forget to come out next spring," Freddie called to his twin.

"It's spring already," Flossie shouted gleefully, sticking her head out of the leaves. Then she cried, "Oh, Freddie, what's this?"

"What's what?" her brother asked.

"This big thing under the leaves."

Freddie investigated. Beneath the leaves he felt something large and round. In an instant he pulled it out. It was the lost volleyball!

"Here's the ball!" Freddie called, out of breath.

"I found it," Flossie protested, going after him.

"Well, anyway, we both found it," Freddie said.

"Where did you find it?" asked Miss Perkins, taking it from him. Freddie told her.

"Somebody must have kicked it into the leaves

and forgotten about it," said the teacher. "Well, thank you. Now we can start the game."

When the spectators had taken their places and the girls had lined up on each side of the net, Miss Perkins threw the ball into the air, and the game was on.

Back and forth the ball went over the net. Lakeport made a score, then Centre School. Right after the tie, Nan, who was playing close to the net, hit the ball hard. It sailed high into the air and a Centre School girl missed it.

"We're leading two to one!" Bert shouted.

But soon the home team evened the score and went ahead. The game see-sawed back and forth while the people on the benches shouted for one side and then the other.

"Come on, Nan, hit it!" Freddie screamed as he saw his sister race after the ball.

It looked as if Nan were going to hit the ball with all her might, so the girls on the other side of the net drew back a few paces.

But Nan tapped the ball very lightly. It barely cleared the net.

The Centre girls realized they had been fooled, and raced forward to hit the ball back. But they could not reach it in time. The ball fell to the ground just as the game ended. Nan's team had won by a single point!

"Hurrah! Hurrah!" shouted Bert, as Nan's team-mates gathered around and patted her on the back.

Nan was the star of the game, and the next morning there was a story about her good playing in the newspaper.

"I'm very proud of you, dear," said her father as he got up from the breakfast table. "I'd like to have seen you play."

After he had gone, Mrs. Bobbsey said she thought the small twins had better not go to school.

"Why not?" asked Freddie, who did not like to miss a single class.

"Both of you have the sniffles. I'm afraid you are catching cold," replied Mrs. Bobbsey. "You can go back on Monday."

It was during this time that workmen installed a couple of drinking fountains in the school-yard Mr. Tetlow spoke about them in assembly, warning the children not to play with the fountains and squirt water at each other.

"Anybody caught playing with the drinking fountains will be punished," he said.

On Monday the small twins went back to school. During morning recess Freddie and Flossie spied one of the new fountains.

"Let's get a drink," Freddie suggested as he ran towards it.

Danny Rugg saw him. A gleam of mischief came into his eyes.

"Want to see the water squirt, Freddie?" asked Danny, walking up to the little boy. "This is a new fountain. It squirts awful far."

"Does it?" asked Freddie innocently.

"Just put your finger over the hole and turn the water on," directed Danny. "You, too, Flossie."

Danny looked all around, thinking he was not being observed as he gave this bad advice. Freddie and Flossie suspected nothing wrong. They had not heard Mr. Tetlow's warning. The two held their thumbs over the nozzle and turned the water on. Out spurted a fine spray, which shot high into the air.

"This is fun!" Freddie shouted gleefully. "I could put out a fire with this!"

Danny, seeing the success of his trick, walked away from the twins just as Mr. Tetlow came around the side of the school building. The little Bobbseys were so intent on squirting the water that they did not see the principal until he was close to them. They were startled as he called out sharply:

"Freddie, Flossie, stop that! You know this is forbidden. Go to my office at once and wait for me!"

CHAPTER XII

A HALLOW-E'EN PARTY

WHEN Mr. Tetlow entered his office he found Freddie and Flossie standing near one of the windows, watching the other children go to their classrooms. They had been crying a little but had stopped now.

"I am very sorry to have to punish you twins," said the principal, "but I gave strict orders not to play with the water fountains. Why did you disobey?"

"Because, because——" Flossie tried to explain, but she could only give a little sob.

"Because Danny Rugg told us to," Freddie said. "He said it was a new kind of fountain that would spray real high."

"Now be careful and tell the truth," Mr. Tetlow said. He often had heard children blame their offences on somebody else. "Are you sure Danny told you to do it?"

"Yes, sir," said Freddie.

"Didn't you know it was forbidden?"

"No, really we didn't," answered Flossie.

"Why, I told the whole school about it," Mr. Tetlow continued. "I warned everybody not to play with the fountains. Didn't you hear me?"

"No, sir," Freddie said. "Flossie and I were absent Friday. Maybe that's when you told the children."

Mr. Tetlow began to understand. "I will look into this," he said, "and if I find——"

The principal was interrupted by a boy from one of the higher classes, who had come into the office with a note from his teacher.

The principal read the note and said to the boy, "On your way back to your class, George, stop at Miss Hegan's room and have her send Danny Rugg to me." He scribbled the message on a piece of paper.

"Is it about the water?" the boy asked.

"Why, yes," replied the principal. "Do you know anything about it?"

"I heard Danny tell Flossie and Freddie to squirt it," he said.

Mr. Tetlow raised his eyebrows. "Thank you, George. Give this note to Miss Hegan. I want to see Danny at once!"

When the boy left, Mr. Tetlow smiled at the

Bobbseys. "In that case, Danny is the one to be punished," he said. "But if Danny tells you to do anything again, find out whether it's right before you follow his advice.

The principal wrote a note, explaining to the twins' teacher why they were late for class, and Freddie and Flossie left his office. Later on they found out from Bert and Nan that Danny's punishment was that he would have to stay after school for three days. Besides, Mr. Tetlow was going to call on Mr. Rugg, telling him he would have to take Danny in hand.

"I wish I had heard Danny telling you to squirt that water," Bert said. "He did it just to get you in trouble. I'd have fixed him!"

"Oh, please don't get into any more fights with him," Nan pleaded. "He's being punished, and you might get hurt."

Lessons and fun filled the Bobbsey twins' days. Work grew a little harder. Even Freddie and Flossie had to study hard to learn all the new words in their reading book.

It was nearing the end of October when the small twins' teacher asked the class, "Do you know what day is coming soon?"

"Christmas!" one boy exclaimed.

"Yes, that's right. But what day comes before that?"

"Thanksgiving!" cried Susie Larker.

"Oh, yes," Flossie said. "We're having our aunts and uncles and cousins visit us on Thanksgiving."

The teacher waited until they had quieted and said, "But there's something else coming before Thanksgiving. Does anybody know what it is?"

"I do," Freddie shouted. "Hallow-e'en! I know 'cause we're having a party."

At recess all the children began to talk about the party.

"Am I invited, Freddie? May I come, Flossie?" each child asked.

"I guess we'll have about a—a thousand people," Freddie said, and his little friends laughed.

"Well," the teacher said, when recess was over, "we're going to make paper pumpkins, and witches riding sticks and paste them on our windows."

"To scare people with?" Flossie giggled. "I'm going to make some at home, too."

The Bobbseys had a lot of fun preparing for their Hallow-e'en party. First the invitations were prepared. The twins made lists of all the friends they wanted to invite. Then Nan made yellow cards, on which she pasted black witches whizzing through the sky on broomsticks. Underneath Bert wrote:

Witches and goblins can be seen
At the Bobbsey house on Hallow-e'en.
Wear your costume and be there.
You'll have some fun and get a scare!

The invitations were put into envelopes, which the older twins addressed. Freddie and Flossie helped by sealing the envelopes and sticking on the stamps. The small twins took the envelopes to the post office themselves.

"My, what a lot of mail!" exclaimed the clerk at the stamp window, as he watched the twins drop the mail into a slot. "Uncle Sam will have to hire some extra postmen to carry all of that. What's going on?"

"We're going to have a Hallow-e'en party," said Flossie proudly.

Just then Danny Rugg came in to buy some stamps for his father.

"A party, did you say?" he sneered. "I'm coming, too."

"You are not," Freddie cried. "'Specially after getting us into trouble with the water fountain."

"You can't come," Flossie said calmly, "'cause you don't have an invitation."

"Oh, no?" said Danny. "I'll just take one of them out of this pillar-box."

Danny moved over to where the children were

dropping the letters into the slot. The postal clerk saw him and said sternly, "Stay away from there, Danny! Anybody who tampers with the United States mail goes to jail."

This frightened Danny. He bought his stamps, scowled, and hurried towards the door of the post office. Then he turned around and said:

"I know how I'll get even with you Bobbseys for not inviting me!"

Freddie and Flossie dropped all the invitations into the box and went home. When they told their mother what Danny had said, Mrs. Bobbsey replied:

"You needn't worry, children. If Danny were a polite boy, we would have invited him. But I know he would spoil the party if he came."

As Hallow-e'en drew closer, the twins were busy planning their costumes. Bert decided to be a pirate, and Nan a Spanish lady.

"What would you like to be?" she asked Flossie.

"I want to be a fairy—a fat fairy, like Daddy says I am," she replied.

"And how about you, Freddie?"

"Don't you *know*?" her little brother said. "I'm going to be a fireman."

"But everybody will recognize you," Nan said. "Why don't you be a dwarf, or a soldier, or . . ."

"I'm going to be a fireman," Freddie insisted.

"Nobody will know me, 'cause I'm going to wear a mask."

When the costumes had been decided upon, Mrs. Bobbsey helped to prepare them. She turned a dancing costume which Nan had worn when she was a little girl into a fairy's dress for Flossie.

Mr. Bobbsey bought boots for Freddie and a cute fireman's hat made out of heavy cardboard. Freddie began to wear it at once, and his mother was afraid it might become torn before the party, so she made him put it away.

Nan found a box of outmoded clothes in which was a black evening dress of her mother's. By shortening it, she had a lovely Spanish lady's gown. Mrs. Bobbsey gave Nan some old combs with brilliant stones and a piece of lovely lace to wear on her head.

As for Bert, he made himself a pirate's hat out of an old box, and a wooden sword. Nan gave him two golden ear-rings. Bert planned to tie a 'kerchief around his head and stick on a big black moustache. Then, with a black mask, he would be a fierce pirate.

When the costumes were ready, the children turned their attention to decorations. Freddie and Flossie cut out goblins and witches, the same kind they were making at school. Bert and Nan draped the living-room with long rolls of black and orange crêpe paper.

"And here's a pumpkin for you," said their father as he came home from work one night. In his arms he held the biggest pumpkin the twins had ever seen. It was as big as four footballs and as yellow as gold.

"Can we scoop it out right now?" Bert asked excitedly.

"After dinner," their father said. "We'll all have fun making a jack-o'-lantern."

And what fun it was! Everybody got a big spoon, and when Bert cut the top off the pumpkin, the children scooped out the seeds and pith.

"Dig out enough for a pie," Mrs. Bobbsey said, smiling, and they did. Finally it was time to cut the face into the pumpkin.

"Do you want the jack-o'-lantern to laugh or to scowl?" Nan asked.

"Make him laugh," they all said at once, so Bert carefully began to cut out the eyes, nose, and mouth.

"Don't forget the teeth," Flossie said.

Bert did not forget. He made great big teeth, and when the jack-o'-lantern was finished, there stood the biggest grinning pumpkin the Bobbseys had ever seen.

"Let's put a light in it!" Freddie shouted.

Freddie found a flashlight, which he quickly put inside the jack-o'-lantern. Then Mr. Bobbsey switched off the lights. The pumpkin grinned and glowed in the darkness.

"Enough to scare anybody," laughed Mrs. Bobbsey.

Soon the evening of the Bobbseys' Hallow-e'en party arrived. The living-room decorations looked very pretty, and the lighted jack-o'-lantern sat on a table, grinning. There was much excitement as the children put on their costumes. Flossie looked like a real little fairy and Freddie like a miniature fireman.

Bert's outfit gave him the fierce and swaggering look of a bold pirate, the kind who used to kidnap lovely Spanish ladies like Nan.

When it was nearly time for their guests to arrive, the children shut off all the lights except the one in the pumpkin and waited near the front door.

Soon the doorbell rang. Bert let in a ghost.

"Who are *you*?" Bert demanded. But the ghost said nothing, merely flapping his arms in his white sheet.

Next came somebody in a tiger suit, followed by an "old man" wearing a funny rubber mask. Soon the living-room was filled with children wearing all sorts of costumes. The Bobbseys tried to guess who they were. Flossie thought she recognized Susie Larker dressed as a clown, but she was not sure.

For a few moments all the guests stood looking at each other. Some of them giggled underneath their masks.

Then somebody dressed in a Red Devil's suit stepped forward. Bert thought it might be Charley Mason. The Red Devil stood over the jack-o'-lantern. Then, without warning, he bent down and pushed out one of the jack-o'-lantern's front teeth.

CHAPTER XIII

AN UNPLEASANT SURPRISE

"GET away from there!" cried Pirate Bert, as the Red Devil pushed out a second tooth of the jack-o'-lantern.

The masked figure moved away. "I was only fooling," he muttered.

"Well, cut it out," warned Bert.

Mr. and Mrs. Bobbsey came into the room directly afterwards. It was lucky for the Red Devil that they had not seen what had happened. Mrs. Bobbsey suggested that if everyone were there, they would start the games.

"But I suppose you can't play very well with your masks on," she laughed. "So suppose we have a parade first, and Mr. Bobbsey and I will give out the prizes for the best costumes. Then you may unmask."

Mr. Bobbsey had a marching record all ready to play. As the music started, the children formed in line and walked slowly around the living-room and hall.

It was funny the way the little girls, who were not used to the long skirts of their costumes, kept tripping over them. The ghost, who could not see very well through the eye-slits in his sheet, ran right into a table!

"That Red Devil costume is pretty good," whispered Mr. Bobbsey to his wife.

But just as he said this, the Red Devil put out his foot and Fireman Freddie, next to him, fell flat. Bert saw the episode. Angry, he stepped out of line and grabbed the Red Devil by the shoulder.

As he did so, the figure's mask was pulled aside a little bit. It was enough, though, for Bert to recognize the Red Devil as Danny Rugg!

"You weren't invited here!" he cried, letting go of Danny.

In that split second Danny dashed from the living-room into the hall and out of the front door. At once there was great confusion at the party.

"Who was he? What happened? Why'd he leave?" asked several boys and girls.

Bert told them, and everyone was glad Danny Rugg had left right at the beginning of the party. No telling what he might have done if he had stayed another minute!

Finally the children sat down, and Mr. Bobbsey

announced that the costume winners were Cinderella carrying her pumpkin shell and six make-believe white mice, and the funny skeleton with the eyes that lighted up.

Cinderella turned out to be Susie Larker, who received a box of candy. Teddy Blake was the skeleton. As he took off his headpiece and went up to get a harmonica, everyone roared with laughter. Now the skeleton had a live face and could talk!

After everyone had unmasked, the games started. There were so many children that Mrs. Bobbsey divided them into groups. In the hall Mr. Bobbsey took charge of the bowl of water into which the guests would duck for apples. Near him Nan watched over a large pan of flour in which dimes wrapped in wax paper were hiding. Such sneezing as the children went through to pick up the money with their teeth!

In the meantime, the children in the living-room were playing Musical Chairs. A number of chairs had been placed in the centre of the room, and the boys and girls were marching around them while Mrs. Bobbsey played the piano. There was one less chair than there were marchers, so that when the music would suddenly stop and everyone would scramble for a chair, someone was sure to be left out.

Another chair would then be taken away, and so on, until only one was left. Grace Lavine and Charley Mason marched about. Mrs. Bobbsey, her back to the children, kept playing for some time, as the two went round and round the chair.

Suddenly the music stopped. Grace and Charley made a rush for the chair, but Grace got it first and so won the game. Bert handed her a new song record, which she went to play at once.

Just then Snap came into the room and with a bark of welcome turned a somersault. Then he marched around on his hind legs, carrying a broomstick like a gun. Bert had given it to him.

"He wants a prize, too," giggled Flossie.

"An' I'll give him one," said Dinah, who had come in to speak to Mrs. Bobbsey about the food. "A nice big lamb bone with all the trimmin's. Come, Snap!"

The dog followed her willingly, as the children laughed and clapped. And Snap barked so loudly —for he liked applause—that there was noise enough to be heard in the centre of Lakeport!

The games went on. Next came peanut races and then potato scrambles. In the first, each player had a dozen peanuts to be laid at equal distances across the room. They had to be carried one by one to a bowl. The players did very well except John Ford, who was in too much of a hurry and skidded into the fireplace. His clown costume was covered with ashes! Nellie won this race easily.

The potato scramble was a similar game, only it was harder, because each player had to pick up the potatoes on a spoon. This ended in a draw between two brothers, Bill and Frank Hill. Mrs. Bobbsey said they would have to take turns wearing the prize necktie!

Almost before the children realized it, the hour for supper had arrived. They were not sorry, for everyone had developed a good appetite.

"Come into the dining-room, children," invited Mrs. Bobbsey, opening the door.

"Oh!" gasped Nellie. "Isn't it beautiful!"

The long table was decorated with hobgoblins and witches dancing among bright-coloured leaves and tiny chrysanthemums.

At each place was a glass dish of cut-up fruit. But what caught the eyes of all the children more than anything else were two large cakes—one at either end of the table.

"It's like a birthday party!" said Susie Larker.

"And in a way it is," Mrs. Bobbsey smiled. "You see, Flossie and Freddie are going to have a birthday in a little while. I'm afraid we couldn't have another party so soon, so we'll eat their birthday cake tonight!"

On one cake was the name *Flossie*. The other

was marked *Freddie*. The names were in pink icing on top of the white frosting that covered the birthday cakes.

"Oh! Oh! Oh!" cried Flossie, completely surprised. "Isn't it sweet!"

"I guess it is sweet," piped up Freddie. "Dinah always put lots of sugar in cake, don't you, Dinah?"

He looked at the cook, who stood in the doorway, grinning. She had had hard work keeping the surprise from Freddie.

"That's what I did, honey! Plenty of sugar!" she exclaimed. "If anybody's got a toothache, he'd better not eat any, 'cause the cakes sure are sweet."

How the children laughed!

"All ready now. Sit down," said Mrs. Bobbsey. "Your names are at your plates."

There was a little confusion getting seated, because it seemed as if everyone's card was on the opposite side of the table to where he was standing. But Bert and Nan helped the guests, and soon each one was in his chair.

"Can't Snap sit with us for dessert?" asked Freddie, looking about for his pet.

"No, dear," said Mrs. Bobbsey. "Snap is a good dog, but we don't want him in the dining-room. He'll have his own dessert in the kitchen."

"Then may I send him some cake?" asked Flossie.

"Yes. Since it's your birthday cake, I suppose you can give him some, if you wish," said Mr. Bobbsey.

After the children had eaten platefuls of delicious creamed chicken, mashed potatoes, and peas, the twins' mother said Flossie and Freddie might cut their cakes while Dinah cleared the table. They started in at once.

"Here, Dinah," said Freddie, as he put a large piece on his plate. "Please give this to Snap."

"Land sakes alive!" cried Dinah. "That sure is somethin'. You want to make Snap sick? That's enough cake for Dinah and Sam an' Snap all together!"

After Dinah had carried out the last plate, Flossie said, "Now we're going to have ice-cream." She forgot that she was not supposed to tell. "All kinds of fancy things for Hallow-e'en," she added.

Dinah went out on the back porch where the caterer had left a carton containing the ice-cream. She looked around and then came running back to the dining-room. Dinah's eyes were big with wonder and alarm.

"Mis' Bobbsey! Mis' Bobbsey!" she cried. "Somethin' strange has happened!"

"What is it? Someone hurt?"

"No, Mis' Bobbsey, but that ice-cream has just

gone an' walked right off the back porch. The ice-cream is gone!"

The children looked at one another with pained expressions on their faces.

The ice-cream was gone!

CHAPTER XIV.

THE FROZEN BUTTON

WHAT sad faces in the funny costumes! The ice-cream gone! All were silent until Flossie burst out:

"Are you sure, Dinah? Maybe it fell off the back porch."

"No, it didn't, honey. I looked everywhere for it, and it's just plain gone."

"Maybe Snap took it," suggested Freddie, as a last hope. "Once he took my book and hid it. Snap," he called, "did you take the ice-cream?"

Snap ran into the dining-room, barked, and cocked his head as if puzzled.

"No, indeedy, Snap couldn't lift a big package like that," declared Dinah. "It wasn't Snap."

"Then who could it have been?" asked Nan.

"That's what I don't know, child," answered the cook. "I suspect, though, that it was some tramps."

"What makes you think that?" asked Mrs. Bobbsey, startled.

"Sam's been tellin' me 'bout some men what's been campin' out down by the river. Folks have been missin' all kinds of food an' Sam's sure those men took it."

"Then I'd better phone for the police," said Mr. Bobbsey. "And in the meantime, I'll run downtown and buy some more ice-cream."

All this time Bert had been thinking hard. Now he jumped up from the table, saying:

"I'm going to have a look outside. Come on, Charley!" When the boys reached the back porch, he whispered to Charley, "Maybe Danny Rugg is up to some of his tricks!"

"I'll bet you're right," cried Charley.

"Here are some fresh footprints that lead up to the porch and down again," said Bert excitedly. "Let's follow them!"

"All right. But we'll have to have a light."

"I'll get my flash," Bert offered.

He ran to his room for it. As he came back through the kitchen, there was Dinah, looking behind the table, under the sink, in the pantry and all about, hoping that, somehow or other, the ice-cream would suddenly turn up. Bert smiled and went out of the door.

"That's the way the footprints go," Charley pointed out, when Bert joined him.

The faint trail led along the stone walk at the side of the house.

As the boys were about to start, Snap pushed open the back door and raced after them. Bert held the dog's nose down against the footprints and said:

"Find who took our ice-cream, Snap!"

Snap seemed to understand. He sniffed the ground, getting ahead of the boys, who had to depend on the flashlight. At first the trail was easy to follow, for the footmarks were slightly muddy. The ice-cream thief must have been walking over damp ground.

"Maybe by the river," thought Bert. "One of those men Dinah spoke about! We'll certainly have to be careful."

When they reached the pavement in front of the house, the marks turned left, and suddenly the trail vanished.

"Now what are we going to do?" asked Charley, stumped.

Before Bert could answer, Snap barked from the corner of the street. They had forgotten all about him.

"He'll show us," said Bert, and they hurried after the dog.

Snap crossed the street and headed into a weedy field, which had been a nice garden during the summer but had been neglected. The dog was right. Here were the same size footprints, made only a short time before.

"But here are two other sets!" cried Bert suddenly. "The ice-cream thief met two other people."

"We'd better watch out," said Charley. "Three against two isn't very good."

"You're right," Bert agreed. "But don't forget, we have Snap."

The smart dog was forging ahead. And he was going straight to the river!

Charley began to grow nervous. He wanted no part of a tilt with three bad men!

"Maybe we'd better let the police find the ice-cream," he said.

Bert did not agree. "We have a head start, and maybe we can save some of the ice-cream."

"Let's just scare the men and not go too close," Charley suggested.

The boys pushed on after Snap, who seemed to be very excited now. He was whining and running back and forth. Finally he came and stood beside Bert, wagging his tail furiously.

"I think we must be close," said Bert.

"What's that over there?" asked Charley, pausing and pointing to a building ahead.

"Richter's old barn, remember?" answered Bert. "Listen! I think I hear voices!"

There was no doubt about it. Muffled voices could be heard in the distance.

"Maybe they took the ice-cream in there to eat it," whispered Charley.

"We'll take a look," said Bert. "Now, Snap, stay with me and don't bark. Come on!"

He led the way to the big deserted barn.

"I see a light in the barn! Take it easy!" warned Charley.

"And it's moving around," said Bert.

"It's those men, all right," decided Charley. "And maybe they haven't the ice-cream, after all."

"We can soon tell."

"Are you—are you going in there?" asked Charley.

"I think we can scare 'em away and then see what's in there," said Bert.

"But how?" asked Charley.

"We'll make a terrible racket as if there were a whole lot of us, and maybe they'll run away," suggested Bert.

He began hunting for rocks, and picked up several. Charley gathered an armful.

"All ready!" said Bert, rushing forward.

He let out a fearful yell and heaved one of the rocks against the side of the barn. Charley threw one, and gave a whoop that would have done credit to any Indian going into battle.

"Get 'em!" shouted Bert in a deep, mannish voice, and let fly another rock.

"C'mon, men!" cried Charley, also in a deep voice.

Thick and fast the rocks were pelted against the old barn. Snap had started to bark furiously, and with the boys calling out in various tones of voice, the din was terrific.

"There they go!" said Bert suddenly.

Three figures could be seen running from the barn and heading for the river. In a moment they were out of sight. Bert and Charley began to laugh. Their little trick had worked!

"Come on," said Bert. "We'll see if the ice-cream is in there."

Flashing his light, Bert dashed ahead, followed by Charley and Snap. Into the big barn they went.

"There's our ice-cream," shouted Bert. "Let's see if any's left."

The carton stood in the middle of the barn floor. A hasty look showed that only a few of the Hallow-e'en ice-creams had been taken out.

"There's plenty left!" said Bert gleefully. "We surprised 'em just in time. Now let's get back to the house."

It was a triumphant pair who returned to the Bobbsey home, carrying the recovered ice-cream. And such a shout of delight as went up from

Flossie, Freddie, and the others as they greeted the boys!

Mrs. Bobbsey hurried to the telephone and called her husband at the shop where he was just about to purchase more ice-cream. Then she notified the police, who were already out investigating.

"Did you catch the bad men?" Freddie wanted to know.

"They ran off," his brother said, and told how the thieves had been scared away.

"Goodness sakes alive!" gasped Dinah. "You're certainly smart boys. That's what you are!"

"Oh, Snap trailed the ice-cream for us," said Bert.

As Dinah and Mrs. Bobbsey were unwrapping the little packages that held the fancy ice-creams, the cook uttered a cry. "Look!" she exclaimed. "There's something black in here, Mis' Bobbsey. Wait till I git it out."

Dinah fished for the black thing, and drew it out.

"Why, it's a button—a frozen button!" she exclaimed.

"A button? How did that get in there?" asked Mrs. Bobbsey.

Bert heard the conversation from the dining-room and dashed to the kitchen. He gave one look at the button and exclaimed:

"I think I know! It was dropped by one of the thieves. I'll save it."

"What for?" asked Dinah.

"It's a clue, Dinah," said Bert. "I'm going to see if I can find a button on someone's coat to match it."

"Be careful not to accuse anyone wrongly," cautioned his mother.

It was just an ordinary black button and it would not be easy to find the owner, Bert knew.

Soon the Bobbsey's guests were eating their ice-cream, and discussing its disappearance. Then after the singing of some school songs, the party came to a close, and good nights were said.

"We've had a lovely time!" said Nellie as she was going out of the door, "and such an exciting one, too!" The other boys and girls agreed.

When Bert went to bed that night he laid the button where he would be sure to see it in the morning.

"I'm going to start tomorrow to find out whose coat that came from," he said to himself drowsily.

Although the small Bobbsey twins and Nan slept late the next morning, which was Saturday, Bert was up early. He had no sooner jumped out of bed than an idea struck him. At the party, the Red Devil's costume had had some black buttons on it!

Bert dressed quickly and rushed downstairs. Only his father was at the breakfast table. The boy burst out with his news. Mr. Bobbsey listened, then said:

"You're probably on the right track, son. But if I were you, I wouldn't be hasty. If you ask Danny outright, he'll probably deny having taken the ice-cream."

Mr. Bobbsey's advice was always good, and Bert never failed to follow it. He could not figure out at the moment, however, just how to make Danny own up. Seeing the puzzled look on his son's face, Mr. Bobbsey said:

"I suppose that truthfully the taking of the ice-cream would have to be considered a theft. But I don't believe Danny looked at it that way."

"You mean he was only playing a trick?" asked Bert.

"Exactly. And if I were you," said his father, "I'd play some harmless joke on Danny in return —something that will let him know you've found him out."

"What could I do?" Bert questioned.

His father arose from the table, smiling. "You figure it out yourself. I'm sure you can."

Bert sat lost in thought for several minutes. Then suddenly an idea came to him. Grinning, he went to the telephone to call Charley Mason.

CHAPTER XV

TIT FOR TAT

"WHAT are you making all those pictures for?" Flossie asked Nan. "They're such funny pictures."

"I'm making them for Bert," answered her sister, who could draw very well.

"Is it a secret?" Flossie wanted to know.

"Well, sort of. At least it's a trick," said Nan. "If you'll promise not to tell, I'll let you know what it is."

"I promise."

"Me, too," called Freddie, coming into the room.

Nan said that Bert was sure the frozen button had come off Danny Rugg's Red Devil costume. He was going to get back at him for taking the ice-cream by sending him pictures and a button. Every picture was going to have the same wording on it:

Button, button, who's got the button!

"Which picture are you going to send first?" Flossie asked.

"The Red Devil costume," Nan replied. "You see, it has a place for three buttons, but only two are on it. Bert's going to clip a big button to the picture, and leave it on Danny's porch this evening."

"The button he found?" Freddie asked.

"Oh, no," said Nan. "He'll give that to Danny some day himself."

Flossie and Freddie giggled. "Which is the next picture?" the little girl asked.

"The old barn. Bert's going to stick that picture in Danny's desk Monday," Nan laughed. "Next day he'll get this one I've just finished."

"It's a carton like the one our ice-cream was in," declared Freddie.

They watched Nan in silence as she drew another picture. Then Flossie said, "Ooh, it's a policeman!"

"That ought to scare Danny," laughed Nan.

She said there was one thing Bert wished he could get, but he supposed this would be impossible without giving himself away. The joke would be complete if he could only get hold of Danny's costume.

"And now remember," Nan reminded the small twins as she put the pictures away, "you two promised to keep the secret."

When Bert came in with Charley a few minutes

later, he had a large black button with him. It was larger than the one they had found in the ice-cream.

"We checked with Bill and Harry and Nellie and Grace," said Bert. "They say I'm right about the button on Danny's costume."

"Pretty soon everybody in town will know the joke on Danny," smiled Nan.

"Serves him right," spoke up Freddie.

About two o'clock that afternoon, when Flossie and Freddie were home alone with Dinah, they started to talk over the joke. Just about this time the first picture was being secretly left on Danny's porch!

"Say, Flossie, let's go for a little walk," suggested Freddie.

"Not to Danny's house," said Flossie. "We promised."

"Oh, all right. We'll go the other way."

They told Dinah what they had in mind and promised not to be gone long and to be careful. As they walked down the side street, Freddie said:

"Let's go to that barn where the ice-cream was."

"Do you know where it is?" his twin asked.

"Sure," answered Freddie.

He did, too. The little boy led his sister directly

to Richter's old barn. They walked inside and looked around. There were horse-stalls to one side, with feeding-troughs in front.

Freddie stood on tip-toe to look over the troughs into the stalls. As he did so, something caught his eye.

"Flossie, look!" he shouted.

His twin came running over just as Freddie pulled something red from one of the troughs. He held it up. The Red Devil costume!

"Oh, Freddie!" cried Flossie.

She turned the suit around. On the back were three buttonholes but only two buttons.

"Just like Bert said," she murmured excitedly.

At that moment Freddie happened to look out of the barn door. Who should be coming across the field but Danny Rugg and another boy!

"We'd better hide!" said Freddie fearfully.

"Oh, where, Freddie?" Flossie wailed.

The little boy gazed about. The only good place was the hayloft. Up the little ladder they scooted, dragging the costume with them. The twins got into a corner and lay flat on the floor.

They could not see Danny and the other boy, but they could hear them. When Danny did not find his costume, he went into a rage.

"I left it right here; I know I did," he declared. "Did you hide it?"

"Of course not," said the other boy. "Hey, look! The ice-cream is gone!"

There followed an argument. Flossie and Freddie could not understand it all, but they figured out that Danny and the other boy, knowing the ice-cream would stay frozen in the special carton, had planned to come there that afternoon and eat some more of it.

"Who do you suppose took it?" cried Danny. "When I find out, I'll—I'll——"

"Listen," said the other boy, "don't be dumb and give yourself away."

"I guess you're right," Danny agreed after a pause. Then he laughed. "The Bobbseys'll never find out who took the ice-cream, anyway!"

Freddie made a face as if he were going to laugh. Flossie whispered "Shush", and the boys downstairs did not hear the twins. Danny looked around once more for his costume and then gave up.

"Maybe George took it," said the other boy, as he and Danny went out of the door.

Flossie and Freddie climbed down from the hayloft and skipped all the way home. Then they burst into the kitchen and said, "See what we found!"

Dinah held up her hands in amazement. "Gracious goodness!" she exclaimed. "The Red

Devil what Bert's been lookin' for! I declare, you honey children are reg'lar detectives!"

Bert and Nan came in soon afterwards from the football game they had attended. Their eyes opened wide upon seeing Danny's Hallow-e'en costume.

"Find out if the button matches, Bert," Flossie begged.

Bert ran to the sideboard where he had put the button and compared it with the two on the red suit. It matched!

"Freddie and Flossie, you're swell!" cried Bert.

He could hardly wait for Monday to come so he could slip the drawing of the old barn into Danny's desk in school. Both he and Nan watched when Danny sat down.

How pale he became and how he fidgeted in his seat when he saw the picture! The Bobbsey twins, Charley, Bill, Harry, Nellie, and Grace had a hard time to keep from laughing.

"What's that?" whispered Bill, who sat alongside Danny. "Let's see it."

"Mind your own business!" growled Danny.

The next day Danny received the drawing of the ice-cream carton. For the rest of the week he came to school early and stayed late every afternoon, trying to find out who was putting the pictures in his desk. But he found out nothing, because there were no more pictures.

On Friday about six o'clock the Rugg doorbell rang. When Danny opened the door, no one was there, but a sheet of paper fluttered to the floor.

"Oh!" cried Danny, seeing the drawing of a policeman with the words on it:

Button, button, who's got the button!

"Oh, oh, oh, I don't want to be arrested!" wailed Danny. "Somebody's going to tell the police on me!"

Outside, behind a hedge, two boys chuckled. Danny was being paid back for his mean trick.

Just then Mrs. Rugg came to the door and asked what the trouble was. Her son tried to hide the paper, but she saw it. Danny insisted he did not know what the words on it meant.

"But he'll find out," laughed Bert Bobbsey behind the hedge.

"When?" asked Charley Mason.

"Monday."

Sunday evening the Red Devil suit was packed in a box, Danny's name was printed on it, and the box was left in the corridor just outside his classroom. The teacher found it and brought it in.

"This is very strange," she said, handing the box to Danny. "Suppose you open it."

Danny's hands shook as he untied the string. He was fearful of what might be inside, but he did not dare disobey. He was relieved that it was nothing worse than the costume. The suit had been packed so that the place where the button was missing was very noticeable.

"I—I lost this on Hallow-e'en," said Danny, and the teacher seemed satisfied with the explanation, but all the pupils in the class who had been to the Bobbsey party were winking at each other and grinning.

Danny was very uncomfortable and made a lot of mistakes in arithmetic and geography. Finally the teacher said he would have to stay after school to make up the work.

By this time he had begun to suspect Bert Bobbsey, and he longed to give him a beating. But he was afraid to try it just now.

"Maybe I can get Bert in trouble some other way," he thought.

Before he figured anything out, Danny received one last reminder of the ice-cream episode. In Danny's desk the next day was a printed note. It said:

If you will stop at Tony's after school, he will give you something.

Danny's curiosity got the better of him, and as

soon as school was over, he headed for Tony's. This was a sweet and ice-cream shop about a block away.

When he arrived, the place was full of children. As Danny stepped up to the counter to ask what Tony had for him, all eyes were upon the bully.

CHAPTER XVI

TURKEY DAY!

DANNY did not have to say a word, because on the counter stood a cardboard sign that read:

FOR DANNY RUGG

Back of it was a tall-stemmed glass heaped up with vanilla ice-cream. On the top, like a cherry, lay a black button!

As Danny gazed at it, there was complete silence in the shop. A strange expression came over the mean boy's face. Then, keeping his eyes lowered, he turned and hurried to the street. Bert removed the sign and the button.

At once, the silence in the shop changed to shouts of merriment. Poor Tony, who had not known about the joke, wondered what had happened. But no one told him. The fun was for certain pupils of Lakeport School only.

"Danny didn't take the ice-cream this time," laughed Charley, "so I'll eat it."

"Bert, you can keep the button for a souvenir," suggested Nellie.

For nearly two weeks Danny was so good that the other boys and girls hardly knew him. Even his particular friends began to tease him about being a sissy and not getting square.

Then one day Danny and three other boys decided to try something. They knew that on days when the morning play-time was held outdoors, Mr. Tetlow came out of a side door and watched the pupils. The boys knew this because once they had tried having a smoke there and had nearly been caught.

"I'll fix Bert Bobbsey," said Danny boastfully.

As the boys reached the playground, Danny told Bert they knew a good new game.

"Come over here and we'll show it to you," urged Jim, one of the boys, who was a new pupil.

Reaching a spot near the side door, he halted and took a packet of cigarettes from his pocket. He pulled one out, lighted it, and handed it to Bert.

"Here," he said, as Bert did not take the cigarette.

"I don't smoke," replied Bert coolly.

"Yah! You're afraid!" sneered Jim. "Cigarettes can't hurt you. It's only cigars and pipes that do."

"I'm not afraid of anything!" said Bert. "But I don't want to get sick. Besides, I said I wouldn't smoke before I'm grown up and I won't."

"Aw, come on!" urged Jim. "Don't be a sissy."

"No," said Bert firmly.

Suddenly Jim leaned down, put out the cigarette, and ran off. So did Danny and the others.

An instant later Bert knew why. Behind him Mr. Tetlow opened the door. For more reasons than one, Bert knew he had been wise not to take the cigarette!

Danny and Jim stood off at a distance looking at Bert and laughing between themselves. Bert knew that they were laughing at him, but he did not care.

That afternoon Mr. Tetlow called a special assembly of the older boys in the school. He said that after play-time he had found a recently smoked cigarette on the playground. The principal asked who was guilty, but no one owned up.

"I want to say a word about cigarette smoking," went on Mr. Tetlow. "There can be no doubt but that it is very harmful for a growing boy to smoke. I shan't go into details, but if you expect to be good in sports, you can't fill your lungs with smoke.

"And I want to add," said the principal, "that not only is cigarette smoking harmful to youngsters, but it is dangerous. Many bad fires have been caused in that way. If I find any of my pupils smoking at school or carrying cigarettes around with them, they will be severely punished. You may go now."

There was considerable talk among the boys after Mr. Tetlow had dismissed them. Bert noticed that Danny and Jim looked rather frightened as they talked together on their way back to class. What they said he could not hear, for they spoke in whispers. Perhaps they were afraid he would tattle!

Nothing more was heard of the smoking for several days, and it was soon forgotten in the press of school work, sports, and plans for the Thanksgiving holiday.

And such preparations as went on in the Bobbsey household for Thanksgiving! Dinah was busy from morning until night for a week before the big day. Every room received a thorough cleaning. Pans of cookies were baked, in preparation for the guests.

"Are all six people coming?" asked Freddie.

"Yes," his mother replied. "Uncle Daniel and Aunt Sarah and your cousin Harry from the farm——"

"I'm glad Dorothy is coming, too," added Flossie. "She's lots of fun. And I like her mummy and daddy."

"Yes, Aunt Emily and Uncle William are good company. We ought to have lots of fun. They're arriving Wednesday evening and staying until Sunday."

"Goody, goody," said Flossie, then added wistfully, "Only I wish we had some cousins as little as us."

When the twins made inquiries at dinner that evening about the turkey they were to have for Thanksgiving, Mr. Bobbsey said it would be the biggest he could buy. And then he asked the children if they knew how turkeys got their name. None of them did.

"Well, way back in the sixteenth century two countries sent big birds to Europe. One country was Turkey, the other Mexico. The Europeans had never seen either kind of bird before, and got mixed up as to where they had come from. So the big Mexican bird was named Turkey by mistake."

"And why do you call him a gobbler?" asked Freddie. "'Cause he eats so much?"

"Probably," smiled his mother, and added teasingly, "That's only the daddy turkey, you know. The daddies always eat more than the mummies."

"Oh, do they?" laughed Mr. Bobbsey. "And I suppose they're naughtier, too. Wild daddy turkeys try to destroy the eggs with the baby turkeys in them!"

"And the mother turkey has to hide them," said Mrs. Bobbsey. "But after the babies hatch out, their daddy is very good to them."

"Just like our daddy is," said Flossie, loyally.

"And just as he is to lots of other people," her mother spoke up warmly. "When Daddy heard about several families in Lakeport who have had hard luck this winter and weren't going to have the kind of Thanksgiving dinner we are, what do you think he did?"

"Bought them turkeys," guessed Nan.

"Yes," said Mrs. Bobbsey, "and celery, cranberries, sweet potatoes, onions, turnips, everything! And we'll send them mince-pies made by our own Dinah Johnson."

All the twins thought this was wonderful, and Flossie got out of her chair to give her daddy a big hug.

"Well, that's nice, Fat Fairy," he said, though he was embarrassed by all the family's praise.

Flossie then ran into the kitchen to say a special thank you to Dinah.

"I'm glad to do it, honey child," said the cook. "An' I'm not forgettin' this family, either," she added. "Dinah's got a surprise for you."

The Bobbseys' relatives from the farm and from

the seaside drove up at exactly the same time the night before Thanksgiving. Flossie and Freddie had gone to bed early, because they wanted to be up at the crack of dawn to watch Dinah and see what the surprise was to be. But the others welcomed their guests with hugs and kisses and handshakes.

"Isn't this exciting!"

"I'm so glad you can stay with us for several days."

"Wait until I tell you about our trick on Danny!"

And so it went, until everyone was breathless from telling the latest news. In the morning Flossie and Freddie came in for their share of the excitement.

"How's Downy?" Freddie asked Dorothy. "Is my duck all grown up?"

"Oh, no," his cousin laughed. "But he will be when you come to visit us at the seaside next summer. I'm glad you left Downy with me. I have lots of fun with him. He rides in my donkey cart with me up and down the beach."

Freddie wished he might ride with his pet duck, too, before next summer. He had not wanted to leave it at the Minturns' home, but his mother had decided Downy would be happier there where he had a pond to swim on, than he would be at the Bobbseys' Lakeport house.

During the morning Nan and Dorothy went to call on some of Nan's friends. Dorothy was well liked because she said such funny things.

"I wish you could stay here longer," Nellie Parks said to her.

"It would be nice," Dorothy answered, "but I'm afraid the poor old ocean couldn't get along without me. I tried to bring it with me, but there wasn't room in the car."

The other girls laughed, and in fact there were giggles and jokes at each house, until it was time for Nan and Dorothy to go home.

Finally the family assembled and went into the dining-room. How attractive the centre-piece was —a mountain of fruit! Peeking out from one corner were two baby turkeys.

"They're not real, of course," Freddie told himself, although they did look lifelike.

As soon as everyone was seated, the twins' father said grace. Then everyone started eating the first course—tomato soup. Freddie was halfway through his, when he happened to glance at the table decoration.

One of the turkeys was moving! A second later the other turkey opened his mouth wide!

"L-Look!" cried Freddie. "They're *real!*"

CHAPTER XVII

THE RACE

FLOSSIE'S eyes grew big as doughnuts as she discovered the baby turkey was moving.

"Mummy, it's real!" she shrieked, bouncing up and down in her chair.

Dorothy put her big white napkin up to her face and when she did, the other turkey with its mouth open seemed to say:

"Uhr whee, uhr whee, uhr whee!"

"Get 'em before they fly away!" Flossie cried, amid the laughter of the older children and the grown-ups.

Before anybody could stop him, Freddie kneeled upon his chair, reached over the table, and grabbed one of the turkeys. Then he looked more surprised than ever.

"It's not alive after all," he said, lifting the turkey off the tablecloth. "Look, it's 'tached to a hose!"

"Oh, Dorothy, it's another one of your tricks," giggled Nan.

The hose was really a thin rubber tube which ran from the turkey to a tiny rubber bulb in Dorothy's hand. When she squeezed the bulb, air was sent through the tube to a gadget inside the turkey, making it walk. Another tube to the second turkey made it open its mouth.

"And you made him talk," said Flossie. "Please, will you give me one of the turkeys?"

"Sure," her cousin answered. "Freddie can have the other one."

"Thanks, Dorothy. You think of the funniest tricks!" Freddie chuckled. "And our Snap does funny tricks, too," he added. "I'll show you."

"Not until we've finished dinner," Mrs. Bobbsey spoke up. "We still have pumpkin and mince-pie coming."

"And Dinah's s'prise," said Flossie.

Her mother rang a tinkling bell and Dinah came into the dining-room.

"We'll have the dessert now," said Mrs. Bobbsey, smiling.

Sam helped Dinah clear the table and bring in the dessert. The cook had told no one what the surprise was to be, so everyone watched in eager anticipation.

At last Dinah carried the surprise in on a large tray. For a moment the diners thought another turkey was being served to them. But as the cook set the gleaming golden bird on the table, Mrs. Bobbsey exclaimed:

"It's made of ice! Dinah, this is a wonderful surprise!"

"Perfectly magnificent," spoke up Aunt Sarah. "How in the world did you get it that colour?"

"That's my secret!" chuckled Dinah happily.

There were "oh's" and "ah's" from everyone at the table. Dinah beamed proudly at all the praise, then pointed out that the bird had a hollowed-out back, in which there was ice-cold ginger ale for everyone to top off the meal.

She brought in some pretty glasses, and Mrs. Bobbsey served out the drinks. Uncle Daniel had two glasses of the ginger ale, declaring:

"This is the finest Thanksgiving dinner I've ever eaten!"

All the others said the same thing. As they arose from the table, Freddie groaned. "Mummy," he said, "it's awful how tight my clothes got," and everybody laughed.

"I had to open my belt," Uncle William confessed. "I won't have to eat again until next Thanksgiving!"

"Now I'll show you Snap's new trick," Freddie

called out as everybody reached the living-room. "Here, Snap!"

The beautiful white dog was in the kitchen, waiting for Dinah to give him his Thanksgiving dinner. When he heard Freddie call, he ran in to him. Freddie held up a finger and Snap sat down.

"Go get your dancing partner," said Freddie.

Snap bounded upstairs, while the little boy started a dance record playing. Snap returned with an old rag doll in his mouth. He dropped it at Freddie's feet.

The little boy held up the doll and said, "Dance, Snap!"

The dog stood on his hind legs and wrapped his front paws around the rag doll. Then he hopped around the room, dancing with the doll!

Everybody clapped to see Snap's new trick, and the dog barked twice, as if to say, "Thank you!"

After Snap had finished performing, the Bobbsey twins and their cousins took a long walk in the brisk autumn afternoon, and played games for the rest of the day. Everyone was glad to go to bed early.

The whole week-end was a jolly one, and Snap seemed to have as much fun as the others. When the guests were preparing to leave Sunday afternoon, they all said they hoped the children could always keep Snap.

"Have you heard from the circus, Richard?" Aunt Emily asked Mr. Bobbsey.

He replied that there had been no news. Nothing had been found out about either Snap or Snoop, the lost cat.

"And the lovely silver cup that was given us at the seaside is still missing," Mrs. Bobbsey said with a sigh. "I do hope we'll get it back some day."

After many good wishes had been exchanged, the Minturns and the Bobbseys from Meadow Brook left for their homes, saying they hoped all of them could be together again for Christmas.

On Monday everybody went back to school. Towards the end of the day, Nan looked up from her arithmetic book and gazed out of the window.

"Oh, look," she whispered suddenly to Grace Lavine, "it's snowing!"

Nan was so excited that her whisper was louder than she had meant it to be. Several other children around her heard it, too, and soon the whole class was looking outside.

What a buzz of excitement there was!

"Take a good look, children," smiled their teacher kindly, for she remembered how thrilling the first snow of the year had been to her when she was a girl and went sledding.

The children ran to the windows for a few

minutes, then returned to their seats, and the lesson continued.

The flakes were coming down faster every minute. There was something about them that made Nan feel sure this would be more than a flurry. A real snowstorm!

Bert could hardly keep his mind on his work. He kept thinking about the bob-sled he and Charley Mason had not finished. So when Bert was called upon to recite, he did not know the place and had to sit down.

The snow was falling more thickly when school ended. The flakes were not so big, but there were more of them, and they blew in drifts along the kerbs.

There was enough wet snow for the children to make a few snowballs, and they began to throw them at each other. Danny Rugg, seeing a chance to pick on someone smaller than himself, packed a hard snowball and pitched it at Freddie Bobbsey.

Bert, who had his eye on Danny, caught it before it hit Freddie. He threw it back at Danny, hitting him in the neck.

"Hey! What are you doing?" demanded Danny angrily.

"The same as you are," Bert shouted back, as Danny reached inside his collar to brush out the melting snow.

"It's going to be swell sledding tomorrow," Bert said to Charley Mason. "We'll have to finish that bob-sled in a hurry!"

"All right. Let's work on it now."

Soon the sound of scraping sandpaper and the odour of paint and varnish came from the Bobbsey garage loft. It continued into the evening. By nine o'clock the bob-sled was finished. Bert and Charley stood back and surveyed it fondly.

"She ought to be the speediest thing going," Charley predicted.

"Especially after Dad showed us how to make those new-style runners," Bert said.

"We ought to have a name on it," Charley suggested.

The boys decided on *Blue Comet*, and Bert printed the name on one side of the bob-sled in blue paint.

The snowstorm kept up all night. Bert set the alarm-clock for early the next morning, and when he awoke, a big blanket of white covered the earth.

Without waking the rest of the family, Bert dressed quickly in warm clothes, put on his boots and met Charley Mason at the garage.

"We'll give the *Blue Comet* a trial run without anybody knowing about it," Bert said, his breath making clouds of frost as he spoke. "The paint's dry enough."

"We're sort of like test pilots, aren't we?" Charley grinned.

They pulled the bob-sled to a hill in the public park, and set off down the slope.

"She's fast, all right," Bert shouted gleefully.

The *Blue Comet* whizzed down the hill, its long runners swishing through the light snow.

"The speediest bob in Lakeport," Charley said with a long whistle, as they reached the foot of the hill. "I wish we could stay here all day and not go to school."

"So do I," said Bert.

The boys went home and put the *Blue Comet* back in the Bobbseys' garage.

It seemed to Bert as if school would never end that day. But finally the closing bell rang, and he and Charley hurried to the Bobbsey house.

As the boys hauled the *Blue Comet* from the garage and started for the hill, a crowd of children followed to look at it. Most of them admired it, but a few laughed at the home-made bob-sled, which was not as trim as those in the shops.

"She'll never coast," sneered Jim, Danny's new friend. "Here come a sled than can!" he shouted.

Danny himself came into view pulling a fine new bob after him.

"Danny's is the fastest thing on the snow,"

declared his buddy George, who was helping Danny to pull the sled.

"We think ours is fast, too," Bert said. "Do you want to race?"

"Sure," said Danny, nearing the top of the hill. This caused much excitement. The sleds were the largest ones in the neighbourhood, and everybody clamoured for a chance to ride down the hill, especially since this was to be a championship race.

"Come on, Nan! Come on, Bill!" Bert called. His twin and several friends climbed aboard the *Blue Comet*.

Danny, meanwhile, had found no trouble loading his bob-sled. When he was ready, he taunted Bert:

"We'll wait for you at the bottom of the hill!"

"By the time you get there, I'll be halfway up again!" Bert flung back.

"That's what you think!" sneered Danny.

With Bert and Danny steering, the sleds were pushed side by side. An older boy held up his hand as a signal, then cried out:

"Ready! Set! Go!"

CHAPTER XVIII

A NARROW ESCAPE

WITH the word "go", the two boys who were to sit at the rear of each sled gave the bobs a mighty push and hopped on.

"There they go!" shouted the onlookers as the two bobs started down the steep hill.

"Danny's ahead!" shouted one of his friends.

"No, Bert is!" retorted another boy.

As a matter of fact, both were even in the race and remained in this position for several seconds as they went whizzing down the hill. On and on they flew, gaining speed on the hard-packed snow.

Gradually Bert's bob forged a little ahead, and his heart pounded, for he felt that he was going to win. He leaned a little to the left to gain extra momentum.

Bert was so close to Danny now that he could have reached out and touched him. Then, inch by inch, Danny's sled gained and started to pass the *Blue Comet*.

"Can't you beat him, Bert?" shouted Charley Mason, who was seated behind Bert.

"I'm trying," Bert said, his jaw set.

Danny overheard what the boys were saying. He turned his head to one side and shouted, "You'll never beat me with that old piece of junk!"

Just then Nan, who was sitting behind Charley, saw that the snow was smoother on the right side of the hill.

"Steer over, Bert!" she called. "You'll go faster over there!"

By this time Danny's sled was a length ahead, and Bert had no trouble steering over to the right on to the smoother part of the hill. At once the *Blue Comet* picked up speed.

In another few seconds Bert was nearly even again with Danny, but now on his right side.

"Look out where you're going," Danny shouted, shaking his fist. "This is my side of the hill."

"You don't own the hill," Bert called back. "Nobody's bothering you!"

"You'd better not run into me," Danny yelled.

This reminded Bert of the winter before, when Danny had run into him and broken his sled. But he did not mention it.

Faster and faster zipped the two bobs. A crowd

at the bottom of the hill, and a number of coasters cheered as Bert's home-made sled gained on Danny's. The *Blue Comet* now was going so fast that the riders clung to the sides of the sled. The wind, rushing by, nearly took their breath away.

"He's passing us, Danny! He's passing us!" shouted Jim, sitting behind Danny.

"Oh, he is, eh? Well, he won't for long!" Danny turned his sled and it nearly swerved into Bert's.

"Look out!" Nan cried. "You'll wreck us!"

"Keep on your own side, then," shouted Danny.

His unsporting trick did Danny no good, however, because Bert, who had had to pull over to avoid being hit, found it even better going.

"Better watch out, Danny," warned another of his riders. "Bert's passing us now."

"It's only a spurt," came the reply. "We'll soon be at the bottom of the hill and win."

On swept the *Blue Comet*. Danny was furious. He thought that if he switched in behind Bert, he might go faster on the other side of the *Blue Comet*. Danny pulled sharply to the right, and the bob nearly hit the back of the other sled.

"Watch out!" Charley shouted.

"I've got a right here," Danny screamed, but the whistling wind drowned out his reply.

Bert did not swerve. He held straight to his

course, and the white stretch of snow between his and Danny's sled became greater and greater.

"We're going to win!" Charley shouted.

By this time the bottom of the hill was not far off. Danny became wild with anger. He decided to steer his sled over into Bert's track. Then, if he could gain speed, he could still win.

Danny jerked his steering-gear, but jerked it too fast. His sled teetered to one side. The riders lost their balance.

"They've upset!" cried Charley, who had glanced back to see where the other sled was.

Bert, of course, kept his eyes straight ahead as a bob-sled captain should, and did not see Danny's riders flying off and the sled turning over in the soft snow on the side of the hill.

"Oh!" exclaimed Nan. "I hope nobody's hurt!"

Before she could say any more about the accident, the *Blue Comet* had flashed past a row of trees at the bottom of the hill, which was the finishing line. With a crunching sound, the bob-sled gradually came to a stop and everybody hopped off.

"Hurrah!" shouted Freddie Bobbsey, who stood with his little sled at the bottom of the hill. "We're the champs. We beat Danny!"

Bert, Charley, and two other boys pulled the sled up the hill to the spot where Danny had overturned. He had picked himself up, and strode over to Bert.

"We won," Bert said, grinning, when he saw that no one was hurt. "Sorry you had a spill."

"You didn't win," Danny snorted, shaking the snow out of his cap. "We didn't finish the race."

"We couldn't help that," Charley said.

"I'd have won if I hadn't turned over in your tracks, Bert Bobbsey!"

"You were beaten fair and square," shouted Frank Cobb, who had ridden with Bert.

"All right," Bert said. "I'll race you again."

"Oh, no, you won't," Danny sneered. "I wouldn't race my new bob against that old wreck of yours again."

"'Cause you know you'd lose," Charley shouted.

"My sled's better," growled Danny as he plodded off, but he was not fooling anybody. All the children on the hill knew who had the fastest bob-sled in Lakeport.

The Bobbseys coasted the rest of the afternoon. Freddie and Flossie went down with their brother and sister several times, and once Nan filled the sled with girls, and steered it. She made almost as good time to the bottom of the hill as her twin had.

In the days that followed, it grew very cold. Workmen cleared the snow off a pond in the park. As soon as the red-ball flag went up, the ice became dotted with children. Bert and Nan were good skaters. They could make figure-eights, grind the bar, and do other tricks.

"Let's skate backwards, and play follow-the-leader," Bert said to his friends one day.

"Okay."

Bert set off backwards, glancing over his shoulder now and then to see that he did not run into anyone. Three other boys followed him. As they went skimming in a circle on the pond, Bert saw Freddie and Flossie, who had double-runner skates and were practising near the edge of the ice.

"Oh, look!" Freddie shouted suddenly.

Bert's runner had hit a deep nick in the ice and he went flying head over heels. He landed on his back and skidded about twenty feet, then scrambled to his feet.

"Wow!" he exclaimed.

"Do it again, Bert," his brother cried gleefully, thinking it was a trick.

Bert skated over to his small brother, brushed himself off, and said, "If I did that trick again, I'd probably land in the hospital!"

Nevertheless, Freddie insisted his brother was the fanciest skater on the pond, and the next day told his teacher how Bert could skate backwards and fly through the air.

The skating lasted only a few days, because a

warm spell set in. The ice on the pond became slushy, so the red-ball flag came down, and the Bobbseys returned to sledding again.

"Let's go to the park hill," Nan said one afternoon.

"Can't," Bert replied. "The snow has melted off the middle of it."

"I know a good hill," cried Nellie Parks, who was playing with Nan. "The one near the pond."

"Oh, that's where I smashed up my iceboat last year," said Bert. "I hope we don't get into any trouble over there this time."

Charley Mason joined them and the four set off. After a long trudge they came to the pond and climbed the hill. It was not so long or steep as other hills in the neighbourhood, but near the foot it dropped away sharply to the pond.

"We'll coast down to this flat place and I'll turn," Bert said. "It won't be a fast ride, but it'll be fun."

The children pulled the bob-sled to the top of the hill. Bert took the front seat. Next came the two girls, and Charley Mason brought up the rear.

"Give her a good push, Charley," Bert shouted when all had taken their places. Charley did, then hopped aboard.

"This is like a slow freight compared to our express service the other day," he grinned, as the sled went slowly down the hill. The heavy bob left deep tracks in the soft snow.

"I think a turtle could beat us," laughed Nellie. "Get off and push, Charley!"

But the sled was actually going faster than Charley could push, and finally they stopped on the flat space.

"All off the molasses special!" Bert laughed. "Maybe if we use the same ruts next time, we'll go faster."

The twins and their friends pulled the sled up the hill once more. Nan noticed that the wind was getting stronger and it seemed to be much colder.

"Just like the weather-man said it would," Charley informed them, when Nan mentioned this. "This morning's broadcast said it would get very cold by late afternoon."

As the temperature dropped, the snow hardened, and the coasters enjoyed faster rides.

"One more ride before we go home," Bert said finally, as the late autumn afternoon began to darken into evening.

When the children reached the top of the hill, Bert said, "Charley, why don't you steer the last ride?"

"Okay, pal."

Charley sat down in front, Bert rushed the bob-sled hard, and off they went down the hill. This time the snow was even harder and they whizzed towards the foot.

"Turn her now, Charley," Bert shouted, as they neared the pond.

Charley tried to, but nothing happened.

"It won't move!" he cried in alarm.

The sled kept on its speedy course towards the pond.

"The steering-gear's frozen!" Charley shouted. "We'll go over the bank."

Nan and Nellie screamed at the thought of hurtling down the steep embankment and on to the ice of the pond. Bert Bobbsey saw that there was only one thing to do.

"Jump!" he shouted.

CHAPTER XIX

BERT IN TROUBLE

HELTER-skelter went the four children off the sled, and just in time. A moment later the *Blue Comet* shot over the embankment.

Bert was the first to pick himself up. Charley and Nan followed.

At the same moment they saw Nellie lying in the snow. She was slumped against the foot of a near-by tree.

"Oh!" gasped Nan, rushing forward. "Nellie's hurt!"

Charley was terribly frightened. He felt responsible for the accident. What if Nellie were badly injured!

"Nellie! Nellie!" Nan cried, kneeling beside her friend.

Slowly Nellie opened her eyes. She seemed dazed and still did not move. Then, just as Nan was wondering if they should carry her quickly to the nearest house, Nellie stirred and sat up.

"How do you feel?" Nan asked her.

"A-all right," the other girl replied. "I bumped —into the tree."

Fortunately Nellie had not hit her head against the trunk and in a few minutes she insisted she felt like herself again. Nan spied an overturned bench and stood it up. She suggested that Nellie sit down and rest before starting home.

As soon as the boys found out Nellie was all right, they started down the embankment to retrieve the bob-sled. As Bert jumped into the snow, not realizing it was a drift, he disappeared up to his chin.

"Look out!" he warned Charley.

"Want any help?"

"I guess I can make it," Bert replied, and struggled out of the snow.

He managed to get to a safer spot, but the descent was treacherous. There were rocks which were now snow-covered. Bert and Charley slipped and slid, finally reaching the snow-covered pond.

The bob-sled lay upside-down about fifteen feet out.

"Maybe the pond isn't safe to walk on," said Charley.

Bert agreed, and the boys wondered what to do.

Looking around, Bert saw a long tree limb which hung out over the pond. The end of it was only a few feet from one corner of the sled.

"I'll crawl out on that limb," Bert offered, "and see if I can reach our *Blue Comet*."

Up above, the two girls watched the little drama. Both kept their fingers crossed. Nan's twin pulled himself slowly along the ice-covered limb, which creaked and groaned as he came nearer the end. Everyone hoped it would not break off! But the limb was sturdy and Bert continued inching his way along.

Finally Bert straddled the limb, held on with one hand, and leaned over with an outstretched hand toward the bob-sled.

"Oh, gee, I can't reach it," he said in disappointment.

On shore, Charley was disappointed, too. "Hey, Bert, I'll throw a stick to you, then maybe you can reach it."

"Good idea," Bert replied.

Charley found a slender tree branch and tossed it to Bert. This did the trick.

Bert fished around until he snagged the end of the rope with the branch, then carefully pulled it toward him.

"Good work!" Charley called. "Can you move the bob?"

At first Bert could not budge the sled even an inch. Each time he tried, the boy nearly lost his balance. He sat still for a moment, trying to figure out what to do. The rope was just too short to reach the shore for Charley to grasp.

"I guess we'll have to leave the bob here and get help," Charley called.

"Wait till I try one more thing," said Bert.

He bounced up and down on the limb until he bent it very low. When it was at the lowest point, he quickly wrapped the rope around the limb, tying it securely. Then slowly he backed up.

As soon as the end of the limb was relieved of his weight, it started to rise back to its normal position. As it did so, the limb gave the bob-sled a yank.

"Oh, swell!" Charley called in praise.

"Your brother's just wonderful, Nan," said Nellie. "I'd never have thought of that in a thousand years."

Once more Bert edged himself to where the rope was tied. He unfastened the loop and slowly pulled the bob-sled along with him as he inched his way to the bank.

Only part of the struggle to get the sled back on the hill had been accomplished. It took the strength of both boys, with Nan's help, to pull it up the steep, rocky embankment. At last they made it, and then looked to see what damage had come to the sled which the boys had worked so hard to build.

"It seems all right to me," said Nan. "Just some of the paint scraped off."

The boys found that one of the runners was slightly bent, and the steering-gear was still frozen. They would have no trouble, however, pulling the sled along.

Bert asked Nellie if she wanted to ride home on the sled. But Nellie said she felt fine and could walk without any trouble.

Bert and Charley worked for the next few days getting the bob-sled in order. Danny Rugg was overjoyed when he heard what had happened to his rival's sled, and went around school asking what anyone could expect of a home-made crate like that, anyway.

Bill thought of going to Danny in defence of his friend Bert, but before he had a chance to do this, something very exciting happened.

It was during a very quiet period directly after play-time that the school gong rang unexpectedly. One—two—three—four. That ring meant a fire drill!

As the ring was repeated, all the boys and girls left their seats. Following instructions, they hurried through the cloakrooms, grabbed their coats, and walked to the hall. Each group proceeded to an assigned stairway and went outdoors.

As the first pupils reached the school-yard, they were amazed to see smoke coming from one of the basement windows. There really was a fire!

As more children assembled, everyone began chattering excitedly. In a few moments the fire-engines clanged up the street!

How excited Freddie Bobbsey was! He wanted to go right into the building with the firemen, but of course he was stopped the instant he tried it.

Nan spotted him and offered to take charge of her small brother since Miss Burns had plenty to do. Freddie asked where Bert was. Nan looked around. He was not in sight.

"I didn't see him after we left our room," she said.

Freddie looked wild-eyed. "Maybe Bert's burning up in there!" he wailed.

Nan quieted her small brother's fears. Bert would have been able to get out of the building as safely as the other children.

"Then maybe he's putting out the fire," said Freddie. "Golly, I wish I could go in there and put some water on it myself."

While his brother and sister were talking about him, poor Bert was having a bad time in Mr. Tetlow's office. The school janitor and the boys' gymnasium teacher had quickly extinguished the blaze in the basement with fire-extinguishers. Then Mr. Tetlow had gone outside and taken Bert back into the building with him.

"The fire downstairs was caused by a cigarette —a Mosswood cigarette," he said. "I am positive the fire was caused by some boy in this school who was smoking in the basement during play-time. Do you know anything about it?"

"No, sir," Bert replied.

Mr. Tetlow frowned. "I'm very tired of dis-obedience and so-called jokes—yes, and even lies among the boys of Lakeport School," the principal said sternly. "This time I mean to get to the bottom of this affair. Bert, will you please lay everything in your pockets on my desk?"

Bert Bobbsey was surprised at the request, but willingly complied. He brought out a penknife, a small flashlight, and a handkerchief. Then sud-denly he felt something unfamiliar in the left-hand pocket of his jacket.

"I said everything," spoke up Mr. Tetlow, as Bert paused.

His face turning pale, Bert laid a package of Mosswood cigarettes on the principal's desk.

CHAPTER XX

A MYSTERY SOLVED

"I—I DON'T know how these cigarettes got into my pocket, sir," stammered Bert Bobbsey.

The school principal looked searchingly at the boy, as if he wanted to be sure he was telling the truth. Finally he said:

"I believe you, Bert, but you certainly must have some idea who is trying to get you into trouble."

"I have, sir," said Bert.

"Who is it?" asked Mr. Tetlow.

Bert did not answer for a few seconds. Then he told the principal that his father and mother had taught him not to accuse anyone falsely. He would prefer to get proof before he named anyone.

"Mr. Tetlow," Bert added, as he suddenly wondered why the principal had asked him to empty his pockets, "maybe you know."

"I don't, Bert," Mr. Tetlow replied, "but perhaps you can tell me who sent this to me."

He opened his top desk drawer, took out a small sheet of paper, and handed it to Bert. On it was printed:

LOOK IN BERT BOBBSEY'S POCKET FOR CLUE TO SMOKING

Bert was too astounded to speak. Although he was suspicious at once, he still did not tell Mr. Tetlow who might have written the note, and who might have caused the fire.

"Of course we shall do our own investigating," said the principal, "but if you find out anything, Bert, I want you to let me know immediately."

"I will, sir," Bert promised.

He was so angry when he left the principal's office that he wanted to do something at once.

"I'd like to accuse Danny Rugg right now!" he said to himself.

Bert's wish was granted almost immediately, for at that moment the dismissal bell rang, and the pupils started home. Bert ran towards Danny's house, then doubled back.

Two blocks from the school he came face to face with Danny, Jim, and George. When they saw Bert's face, the boys guessed something was going to happen. But they pretended not to know this.

"What's the matter?" asked Jim. "Did somebody scare you?"

Bert did not answer. He went straight up to Danny and grabbed the lapels of his coat. The bigger boy was so amazed he did not move. Then, before Danny could do anything, Bert gave him a hard shove, sending Danny sprawling. Jim and George stared, open-mouthed.

"I—I thought you told us you'd never let Bert do that to you," Jim stammered, as Danny struggled up off the ground.

Danny got up, but he was so shaken by Bert's sudden attack that he hesitated, gazing at the Bobbsey boy's ready fists.

"What did you shove me for?" he shouted finally.

"You tried to get me in trouble, telling Mr. Tetlow I started that fire in school with a cigarette," Bert retorted.

"I did not!"

"Go ahead, hit him," George egged Danny on. "Don't let him talk to you like that!"

Danny moved towards Bert, but he had to duck back as Bert's fist flew out and grazed the end of his chin.

"You started that fire," Bert continued. "And you set my father's boathouse on fire, too!" he cried.

"I did not!" Danny shot back. "And if you say I did, you'll get the beating of your life, Bert Bobbsey!"

Still Danny hesitated, but suddenly an idea came to him.

"Say, fellows, you're in this," Danny told his pals. "We were together that night. Are you two going to stand there and take it?"

Jim and George shot startled glances at Danny. This was not their fight. But if Bert were accusing them of the boathouse fire, perhaps they should do something about it.

"Let's all three of us fight him," Jim said suddenly.

Danny's idea of having his friends gang up on Bert was working out!

"You'll do nothing of the kind," suddenly came a girl's voice.

Nan appeared around the corner in time to see the three boys about to pounce upon her brother.

"You can't stop us," Danny sneered.

Nan said nothing. She turned and ran away as fast as she could.

"See? She's yellow, too," George sneered. "When she comes back, she can pick up the pieces!"

With that the three boys set upon Bert with their

fists flying. Bert did not give ground. He hit George on the nose and Jim in the eye, and the two boys dropped back while Danny tussled with Bert.

The pair fell into a clinch, rolling over and over on the ground. First Bert was on top, then Danny.

"Help me!" whined Danny to Jim and George, as he took a breather.

Just as they started in again, there was great shouting. Up ran Charley Mason and Bill Cobb, with Nan leading them.

"There they are," she pointed.

Bert's friends tackled Jim and George. Nan became so excited when Danny gave her twin a hard wallop that she grabbed hold of Danny's hair, pulling it so hard that the boy cried out and let go of Bert.

Suddenly a deep voice boomed above the turmoil, "Stop it, all of you!"

A policeman!

"I saw what happened," he said as he collared Danny and his two pals. "If you must fight, why don't you fight fair?"

"That boy started it," Danny said, pointing to Bert.

"I had a good reason," Bert replied. He told the policeman about the school fire and the

Mosswood cigarettes, and how he had been wrongly accused.

"Fire, eh?" said the officer. "There's been a lot of 'em recently. Maybe you three are at the bottom of it all. Come along with me."

Danny, Jim, and George pleaded with the policeman, but he marched them off to the police-station. Bert, nursing a bleeding nose, went away with Nan, Charley, and Bill.

"Thanks, fellows," said Bert.

During the afternoon session, to which Danny and his friends did not come, Bert was summoned once more to the principal's office. But what a different session this was from the other one!

"Bert," said Mr. Tetlow, "I want to congratulate you. Word has just come from the police-inspector of a full confession from Danny, Jim, and George. They admitted putting the pack of cigarettes in your pocket.

"They also laid a lighted cigarette on the cement floor, knowing the janitor would find it soon and report to me. They didn't count on a breeze blowing it to some oily rags and starting a little fire."

That evening Mr. Bobbsey was hardly inside the front door when the twins started their story.

"Danny's in jail for a million years!" exclaimed

Freddie, who had added his imagination to the story.

"Who's in jail? What's this all about?" Mr. Bobbsey asked.

After Bert had given the details, Mr. Bobbsey said, "I think I'll phone the police-station and see if they found out anything about the fire in our boathouse."

Mr. Bobbsey cautioned Freddie to be quiet while he made the call to the police-station.

The desk sergeant told him a long story.

"Yes. Yes," Mr. Bobbsey said. "Is that so? Well, I'm sorry to hear of boys getting into such serious trouble."

When he put down the telephone, Mr. Bobbsey told his family that Danny and the others had not caused the boathouse fire, but had given a good clue to the person who had.

"The three boys were prowling around the boathouse that night," Mr. Bobbsey went on. "Jim broke a window to get in. They each smoked a cigarette and then left.

"But later on, one of those men whom Dinah told us about—she called them the bad men down by the river—saw the door open and went inside. It was he who started the fire."

Mr. Bobbsey said that the parents of the three boys had been summoned to the police-station, where they had been told that their children needed more strict supervision. Three irate fathers had promised to supply it.

"That's one mystery cleared up," said Bert. "I wish we could solve the one about Snoop and Snap and the silver cup."

CHAPTER XXI

A LETTER FROM FAR AWAY

"IF we could find out who owns Snap, we could offer to buy him," said Mr. Bobbsey.

At this announcement Freddie gave such a whoop and Flossie such a squeal of delight, that their mother put her hands over her ears. Bert and Nan were as pleased as the smaller twins to hear what their father said. But when were they going to learn something about Snap?

"As soon as I hear from the circus manager," Mr. Bobbsey continued, "we may have the answers to all the rest of our mysteries."

But the days went by, and still no word came from the circus. The children grew more and more fond of Snap. He always walked to school with them, and tried several times to go inside the building. But they always sent him home.

One morning Snap helped the small twins carry

some things to school. In connection with their arithmetic, the class was to have a shop project. Each child was bringing tins and boxes of food for the shop shelves.

"To make-believe sell them," Flossie had explained to Dinah after asking for the twins' share of the food.

When Freddie and Flossie reached the school, Snap did not want to give up the bag he was carrying. The playful dog danced around, dodging the children, as if to say, "You've got to take me in with you this time."

Freddie finally grabbed the bag, which tore, and sent Snap home. The dog walked off slowly, looking very unhappy.

The twins carried the food to their classroom and put it on one of the shelves. Nearly an hour was spent on the shop project. The children loved learning addition and subtraction by playing store, and Freddie said that, next to being a fireman, he would like to be a shopkeeper.

When the lesson was over, Miss Burns asked, "What would you children like to plan for assembly tomorrow? It's our turn to put on the programme."

Before anybody could answer, the children's attention was directed to the door of the classroom, which swung open with a bang.

"Snap!" cried Freddie, as the Bobbsey pet bounded in.

The dog walked across the room on his hind legs, jumped to the top of the teacher's desk, and sat up as if begging.

Miss Burns was so startled at first that she could say only, "My goodness gracious!" Then she began to laugh as Snap raised his head and made a low, howling sound.

"Snap's singing," called out Teddy Blake.

"We didn't know he could sing," Flossie giggled. "Oh, Snap, how many tricks can you do?"

Snap kept on singing. The class laughed so much that finally Miss Burns said they would have to be quiet. Mr. Tetlow might come up to investigate all the noise.

"I know what we could do for our assembly programme," Freddie suggested. "We could let Snap do tricks and sing."

"Yes, yes," chanted all the children. "Let Snap sing at assembly."

Miss Burns said that would be very unusual, but then, she was always planning something out of the ordinary for her first-graders.

"All right," she agreed. "We'll let Snap sing. But he ought to have some accompaniment."

"A company of men?" asked Susie Larker, not understanding. "What's that?"

"Don't you know?" Freddie said proudly. "My daddy's lumber-yard is a company of men. I heard him say so!"

By this time Miss Burns was laughing so hard that tears rolled down her cheeks.

"No. No," she said. "Accompaniment means that somebody will have to play an instrument along with Snap's singing."

"Let's have a band," Freddie suggested. "That's more of a company than just one player."

"Very good," the teacher agreed. "That will be our programme. We'll make up a band and play while Snap sings."

The rest of the day was taken up with plans for the First-Grade Band. What the instruments were to be was a secret from the rest of the school, for this was to be a surprise performance.

When they were about to leave school, Miss Burns whispered something into the ear of each child.

"Don't tell anyone," she said. "And ask your mothers to come to assembly. I know they'll enjoy our skit."

When the small twins reached home with Snap that afternoon, they asked Dinah to come into the pantry with them. Then, when they were sure nobody was listening, they told the kind cook of their part in the First-Graders' Band.

"Well, bless your hearts," Dinah chuckled. "I sure will do that! And won't everybody be surprised!"

She rummaged around and very secretly handed the children what they had asked for.

"Run along now, and don't let anybody see them," she said.

That evening Freddie and Flossie invited their mother to the assembly programme. Mrs. Bobbsey said she would be delighted to attend.

"What's the programme?" she asked the twins.

"We can't tell you," they said, and Flossie looked at Freddie and giggled. "But you'll like it, Mother."

The twins did not even tell about Snap's visit to school because that would be giving part of the secret away.

Next day, just before the classes of Lakeport School were to march to assembly, Miss Burns rehearsed the programme. Mr. Tetlow was coming past at the time, and wondered what all the music was about. Glancing through the glass in the door, he smiled to himself and walked on.

Soon it was time for assembly. All the classes filed into the big auditorium. When the pupils found their seats, Mr. Tetlow stepped out on the stage in front of the big curtain.

He welcomed the mothers, who sat in the rear

of the auditorium, then conducted the usual Biblical reading and patriotic songs. At the end, he said:

"Our special programme today will be given by Miss Burns's first-grade pupils. It will be quite different from our usual kind of entertainment, I can assure you."

Three loud chords were played on the piano and the stage curtain went up slowly. What a sight the first-graders made! Every child held a funny little instrument, and they all stood around Snap, who sat on a table.

At a signal from their teacher, the children began to play their school song. As they blew and sawed and hummed into their instruments, Snap lifted his head and sang soulfully. His mournful voice quivered as it went up and down the scale.

"Look what they're playing!" laughed Bert.

"Freddie's beating on our dinner chimes with his little hammer," Nan giggled.

"And Flossie's blowing on the top of a bottle," Grace Lavine laughed.

There were all kinds of instruments in the band. One boy was playing on an egg-slicer, over the end of which he had stretched a piece of tissue paper. His sister was scraping an old knife over a cheese-grater.

Several boys were banging on pie-tins like

cymbals, and one girl was tooting a horn her mother used for squeezing icing on to cakes.

The louder the children played, the louder Snap sang. At first the audience smiled, then everybody laughed until the auditorium resounded.

The programme ended with Snap doing some of his finest tricks. Mr. Tetlow and the other on-lookers declared the performance one of the best they had ever seen.

When the programme was over, Mrs. Bobbsey took Snap home. At once she told Dinah what he had done. The cook put her hands on her hips and laughed heartily.

"That was a howlin' success, sure enough," she said. "Those honey children! What'll they think of next?"

The dog and the music continued to be talked about until Mr. Bobbsey came home that evening. Then all thoughts of the performance went from the twins' minds as he said:

"I have something to tell you all about Snap."

He reached into his pocket and pulled out a letter.

"What is it, Dad?" Bert asked anxiously.

"I received a letter today from Puerto Rico," his father said. "It's from the circus fat lady. I'll read what she says."

CHAPTER XXII

SNOOP RETURNS

THE Bobbsey twins became more quiet than they had ever been in their lives. The letter from the circus fat lady was an important event.

"I'll read the letter to you—every word," said the children's father. "Here it is:

" 'Dear Mr. Bobbsey,

" 'How distressed you must have been upon losing your valuable silver cup and your lovely cat Snoop! When the train stopped so suddenly at the time of the wreck, I saw your silver cup rolling on the floor and picked it up. I did not know the owner, of course, and asked several people. No one knew anything about it, so finally in the confusion I slipped it into my bag.

" 'Later, when I came across it, I wondered how I could find the owner. The circus came to

Puerto Rico soon after that, and has been travelling around ever since. My manager has only just received your letter asking about the cup, or I would have written you before. I will ship the cup to you at once, and I am sorry to have worried you.'"

"Oh, goody!" cried Flossie. "We'll have our nice cup back again!"

"But what is in the letter about Snap, Dad?" asked Nan.

"Here it comes," he said, and read on:

"'When our circus was wrecked, we lost a valuable trained dog. He could play soldier, dance on his hind legs, turn somersaults, and do a number of other tricks. It sounds as if the white dog you have might belong to the circus. We called him Bob.'"

There was a moment of silence after Mr. Bobbsey read this, and then Freddie wailed:

"That must be Snap. Oh, Daddy, you won't give him back to the circus, even if he answers to the name of Bob?"

"Let's see if he does," suggested Mr. Bobbsey, and Freddie brought the dog in.

"Sit up, Bob!" commanded Bert.

The dog sat up, but cocked his head as if surprised. Bert tried several other tricks, using the name Bob. Each time Snap responded.

"I guess that proves Snap is the lost circus dog," said Mr. Bobbsey. "I'll offer to buy him, but I don't want you children to hold your hopes too high."

There was still more to the letter. "Listen," said Mr. Bobbsey, as he went on reading:

"'At the time of the wreck, we picked up a big black cat that joined the circus by mistake. We brought him to Puerto Rico, and I have been teaching him tricks. He must be your missing cat.'"

"Our Snoop!" shouted Freddie. "The fat lady has our cat!"

One Saturday, some time later, a delivery van stopped in front of the Bobbsey house. At last the waiting was over!

"Two boxes for you, Mrs. Bobbsey," said the driver, as he opened his receipt book. "I'll bring them in while you sign."

In a few minutes the man came up the walk with two boxes. One was small. The other was large and had slats at one end. And from this box came a peculiar noise.

"It's a cat!" shouted Freddie.

Quickly the boxes were carried into the house. Bert got a hammer and screwdriver and soon opened the one containing the black cat.

"Oh, Snoop, you precious, precious!" sang Flossie, as he crawled out.

At that instant Snap walked slowly into the room. Instantly Snoop backed into the box again.

"Oh dear!" cried Flossie as she saw the dog. "Maybe they'll fight!"

"I'll hold Snap," volunteered Bert. "Come on, Snoop! Come out!"

"Meow!" cried Snoop, but remained where he was.

It was not until he was sure the dog could not get loose that Snoop came out. He looked about him strangely for a moment, then began to purr, and rubbed up against Flossie's legs.

They all looked anxiously at Snap. The dog glanced at the cat, stretched lazily and wagged his tail. Then with Bert still holding him, the dog walked closer.

The two animals sniffed at each other. Then, to the surprise of all, Snap, wagging his tail in friendly, welcoming fashion, put out his red tongue and licked Snoop.

"He's kissing him! He's kissing him!" cried Freddie.

"Yes, they love each other!" exclaimed Flossie. "They are not going to fight!" and she danced in delight.

Mrs. Bobbsey, satisfied that the two animals would be friends, opened the other box. It contained the silver cup, so long missing.

Mr. Bobbsey came home soon after, smiling.

"I have a letter from the circus manager, and he will sell Snap to us. I have already sent the money. And there is another letter from the fat lady, telling about some of the new tricks she taught Snoop, so you can make him do them."

"Oh, everything's wonderful!" cried the Bobbsey twins in delight.

What a lot had happened in just a few weeks! And more adventures were in store for them at Snow Lodge.

After reading the circus fat lady's second letter, the twins put Snoop through his new tricks.

"I know something!" said Freddie enthusiastically. "We'll put Snoop in school assembly the next time it's our turn!"

Read more of the Twins' adventures in
"THE BOBBSEY TWINS AT MEADOW BROOK"